Alison Lock's first collection of poetry *'A Slither of Air'* was published in 2010 after winning the Indigo Dreams Poetry Collection Competition.

Since then she has gone from strength to strength, and many of her poems and short stories have been published in anthologies, magazines and even a mobile phone app. She also won 1st prize in the October 2011 Sentinel Literary Quarterly competition.

She has an MA in Literature Studies (Creative Writing) from York St John University and was the first Poet-in-Residence at Holmfirth Arts Festival.

ABOVE THE PARAPET

ALISON LOCK

Indigo Dreams Publishing

First Edition: Above The Parapet

First published in Great Britain in 2013 by:
Indigo Dreams Publishing Ltd
132 Hinckley Road
Stoney Stanton
Leics
LE9 4LN
www.indigodreams.co.uk

ISBN 978-1-909357-10-5

Designed and typeset in Minion Pro by Indigo Dreams.

Cover photograph by William Farr

Printed and bound in Great Britain by Imprint Academic, Exeter
*Papers used by Indigo Dreams are recyclable products made from
wood grown in sustainable forests following the guidance of the Forest
Stewardship Council*

For Ian

Thank you to the editors who first published these stories. Some are in slightly different form or have their original titles indicated in brackets:

Erthenta – Highly Commended in the Momaya Press Awards and published in the Momaya Annual Review 2012, also performed for A Word in Your Ear www.awordinyourear.org.uk

The Inventions of Mr Pitikus – Bridge House Publishing ww.bridgehousepublishing.co.uk - thank you for releasing my work early.

Swarm – won 1st Prize in the Sentinel Literary Quarterly Oct 2011 and *Where the Blue Line Fades* won 2nd Prize in the same competition – both published in the Sentinel Champions #10 anthology. *Runner* (Run Boy, Run) – Sentinel Champions #7. *Poetic Licence* – 2nd Prize Sentinel Literary Quarterly July 2012 – Sentinel Champions e-book February 2013.

Map Woman – (Beholder of the Eye) Ether Mobile Quick Reads. www.etherbooks.com

Tweed (The Cemetery Bus) – Journeys and Places – York St John University 2010.

Apple Tree – Onward Anthology. Volume One. *Eggshell* – Onward Anthology. Volume Two.

I would like to thank my family and friends for all their encouragement, especially to Ian, whose support has made it all possible; to my boys, who believe I can do it; and special thanks to Suzanne for her advice and enthusiasm.

CONTENTS

ABOVE THE PARAPET

Ashes for Roses

Only a moment ago she had been enjoying the twist of her spoon in the syrup jar and watching the golden slick drizzle onto her waffle. Now she was meant to be fearful about an environmental crisis dreamt up by the government or the journalists—she had never really understood the difference. Leah could see for herself that everything was just as it had been the day before, the sky almost entirely blue with the exception of a scattering of nimbus wisps, except that today there were no vapour trails playing at Noughts and Crosses and the only sound was a repetition of chirps and peeps that came from a single bird. The garden fork stood perpendicular to the level soil and a robin perched on the wooden handle, its head tilting from side to side as if trying to make sense of something intangible, something more elusive than air.

Leah shrugged, as if to both acknowledge and at the same time dismiss the thought that passed through her head. The paint brush was still where she had left it, balanced on the rim of the tin of paint next to the picket fence. She had almost finished when she had decided to come in, put the kettle on and, more significantly, switch on the radio. Now she wished she hadn't.

'Everyone is advised to stay indoors until the exact nature of the damage is known. Those suffering from respiratory or other breathing difficulties will be issued with a face mask. These will be delivered directly to you. Do not venture outside.'

"I don't believe it," Leah said, "not when my Babes are about to peak."

"Well, it's unlikely to affect us here," replied her brother. "Of course, you could cut them straight away."

"But it's really too early," Leah resisted. "They could spoil."

"Well, they're probably exaggerating," Henry said. "These news reporters do like a crisis. It's what keeps them in a job."

"I can confirm that there has been an explosion of some significance ten miles out to sea from the Elsinor volcano. The impact on the atmosphere is, as yet, unknown."

Leah looked at him quizzically. Henry had always been the apple of their father's eye. 'A practical chap who'll make a fine horticulturalist', Father had always said. As a young child, Henry had helped his father in the greenhouse, sifting through the delicate seeds to find the healthiest ones, planting them into pots, and nurturing them into fully grown plants. His father had high hopes that one day his son would attend the famous Dukes Horticultural College. Consequently, their summer family holidays were spent visiting the great gardens of Europe. After one such holiday their father set about building a glass topped bunker at the bottom of the garden. This was the banana house.

As it happened, Henry never did go to college and he lost all interest in exotic plants or any other kinds of vegetation by the time he was twelve. It was only in the last ten years that his childhood interest had been rekindled and this time it was for roses.

All these years later, it was just the two of them—a brother and a sister living at their parents' home well into their sixties. Leah was often irritated by Henry. He still felt the need to excel at everything whether it was building a new greenhouse, collecting firewood, fixing the car or producing perfect specimens for the County Show. The latter was the unspoken subject; the one that hovered in the air.

The Prime Minister's disembodied voice came from the radio.

"After consultation with the experts and taking all factors into consideration, I declare a State of Emergency."

"This is ridiculous," Leah said, spluttering into her cup of tea.

Since their father had died, Henry and Leah had thrown all their energies into the garden: firstly re-glassing the greenhouse, coating the sheds with wood preserver and mending the fences. Then they turned to the plants. Leah enjoyed pricking out seedlings and placing them into tiny newspaper cones filled with the best compost and once they were a few centimetres tall she would plant them into the well prepared vegetable beds.

They were virtually self-sufficient when it came to fruit and vegetables and in the autumn, their time was taken up bottling and freezing and preserving all the produce. The kitchen became steamed up; rivulets of sweet scented berries ran down the walls, vinegar and citrus permeated the pans, the hob and all the surfaces became sticky with daubs of chutney and jam. Both their faces had a bright boiled glow that lasted for a fortnight making them look thoroughly hearty and rustic. By Christmastime every shelf held the produce of their labours with rows of jars each topped with a chequered cloth and a hand scripted label. There were even pears in brandy.

Now, it was late in the summer and before all the activity could commence it was time to put the finishing touches to the best blooms and produce for the Annual Show. This time, Leah had entered the show on her own behalf. She was to display her favourite roses, the Apricot Babes, a variety that was relatively unknown and not generally popular. She loved the shades and dappled quality of their petals and the scent was as fragrant as a subtle but expensive perfume. The original stocks had been a birthday present from Henry and within a few years of tender nurturing in a loamy soil they had produced a flower that could compete with his more traditional variety. Henry's roses were a constant; a constant source of prize winning pride. He had never actually won first prize and it was a source of frustration to him that it was always Derek their neighbour who received that particular honour. This year he felt confident that there would be no serious competition. Well, almost.

It had taken Leah a lot of courage to announce that she intended to enter the Best of the Roses category.

"I don't suppose they'll be any good, only I do so love my Babes and I might as well... hadn't I..." her voice trailed off.

Henry had shrugged his shoulders.

"Do what you like," he'd said. "Makes no difference to me."

But the gauntlet had been thrown. Leah knew when she heard the squeak of the back door in the early hours that pistols were drawn, so to speak.

Henry approached every task with an exactitude that allowed no errors. It was no wonder that he preferred a perfectly balanced growing medium, a meticulous management plan for lighting and climate control. The old bunker was perfect and as sturdy as it had been when first built. It had two doors, one outer and one inner; so there could be no imbalance of pressure within the inner chamber. It was free of bugs and pests, and not only that, it would take a planet sized meteor shunting the Earth off its axis to affect Henry's little darlings.

Now Leah looked out through the kitchen window. The green shoots of the runner beans were waving from their wigwams. Beyond them were the delicate heads of her Babes; their precious petals protected on all sides by a series of trellises interwoven with clematis and honeysuckle. The roses were set off to their best advantage, thorn free and the most tantalizing shades of orange, cream, and an almost indistinguishable peach; the latter being the signature shade of the Apricot Babes. Their hues gave the far end of the garden an aura not unlike a perfect sunset even in this late morning light. She could almost weep at her dilemma. If she picked them now they would wilt before the show but if she left them until the following day they could be buried under a pile of ash, that is, if she believed what they said on the radio.

"Don't even think about it," said Henry who had an uncanny way of reading her thoughts. "You heard what the Prime Minister said."

The radio voice immediately confirmed the gravity of the situation.

'A potentially poisonous ash cloud is rapidly advancing towards the British Isles and according to our most senior meteorologists it is expected to arrive directly over Central County by 1300 hours today.'

"It's 11 o'clock now." Leah said looking up at the clock. "What are we going to do?"

"What are **we** going to do?" Henry asked. "They're your Babes, so you're always telling me."

Leah's face went white. They both leaned forward, straining to listen to the radio.

'The cloud is likely to meet with a cold weather front from the North when it is predicted that the ash will descend at a low *pressure point – the location has been pinpointed as the town of Melton Hissop in Central County. All the evidence points to this village as the epicentre of the disaster. Those in the affected areas are advised to keep their radios on for further broadcasts.'*

"It must be an April Fool," Leah said. Her voice wavered. "It's got to be, hasn't it? It's like the one about the Martians landing. Except that it's not April 1st..."

"It'll certainly put Melton Hissop on the map," said Henry and he laughed in that laid back way that Leah found very disconcerting.

"It's not a joke, Henry," Leah reminded him.

"Well, it's either a joke or it isn't." Henry looked smug. "You can't have it both ways."

"That's it! That's it!" Leah cried. "I'm not putting up with it!"

"Listen to what the Prime Minister says..." Henry began.

Leah had started for the door before Henry could stop her.

"Sod the Prime Minister," she shouted over her shoulder. "What does he know about roses?"

"I'm not letting you go out there." Henry was using his big brother voice.

He caught the edge of Leah's cardigan just as she grabbed hold of the door handle. At the same moment there was a knocking sound. It came from the other side of the house; then another knock. The two of them froze. Leah slowly let go of the door handle allowing it to rise back into place.

A few moments passed.

"I think whoever it was has gone away," Henry suddenly announced in a normal voice, but even he jumped when the radio bristled back into life.

'Let's go over to our reporter Phil Gibbons at Broomstead Airport. Phil, what's it like where you are?'

There was a crackle as the reporter's connection was lost. There followed some studio talk about the amount of ash that might conceivably fall on Central County. Leah's mood took a turn for the worst. She was beginning to believe the man on the radio.

"They could have given us more warning," she huffed. "By tomorrow the whole garden will be under a ton of cinders."

"Isn't ash supposed to be good for roses?" Henry said.

He seemed to think this was funny judging by the smirk on his face. What would he know about growing roses in a garden when his were grown in an artificial environment that had to be controlled by the hour, the minute, the second? Only last night Leah had heard Henry padding down the stairs in the early hours: Henry's precious babes were about to experience a rainfall of pure filtered water that had been siphoned into a holding tank at one end of the bunker and then sprinkled via a system of shower heads which were positioned at perfect intervals. Oh yes, Henry's roses were primed to put on a perfect display in time for the Show.

The knocking started again, this time at the back door. A familiar outline appeared through the frosted glass.

"Have you heard the news?" It was Derek, their neighbour. "I know you're in there."

He was shouting through the letter box.

"Best to pick them while you can, Leah," he advised.

"Don't you know that you shouldn't be out of doors," Henry shouted. "Go on home. It's not safe."

"Bloody rubbish!" Derek mumbled as he shuffled away. "Only trying to give you some neighbourly advice."

The radio crackled back into action as the reporter on the scene reconnected.

'I'd say a ghost town wouldn't be too strong a phrase, Melvin. There's nobody on duty. Passengers are advised to stay away until they have been contacted by their tour operators. Those who were here last night have been turned away – some are staying at hotels in the vicinity....but most people... have been taken to the Central County Showground where preparations are in hand for the annual flower and vegetable show'

The reporter gave an ironic laugh.

"Oh well, you know what that means don't you?" said Henry, brightening up.

"What?" Was there some hope after all?

"All those tourists that can't get away will be at the Show. They're a captive audience and more to the point the TV crews will be following them around. It'll go national, international, global..." Henry's voice caught on the last word.

Leah could see him now. A Channel 6 News crew: Henry's arm around a plumped up spray of perfect green stems, his cheek against a flawless bloom while he explained to the reporter how he had spent twenty years nurturing his specimens.

'We have information coming in from the Showground at Melton Hissop where we have a reporter on the ground. Hello, hello, Julian, are you there?'

There was a moment's silence. Henry and Leah held their breath.

'Yes, Hello Melvin. It's total pandemonium here. (Crackle,

18

shish.) Some people are already sheltering beneath the trestle tables to protect themselves from the falling ash. I have a family from Nottingham with me now. 'Tell us what happened to you?'

A man was interviewed. There would be no compensation he'd been told. The disaster was considered to be an Act of God.

'The main flower tent has now become a soup kitchen and the army has been called in to help with the organisation. It has been confirmed by the organisers that the Annual Flower Show will be cancelled for this year.'

Leah looked at Henry. In the background they could hear raised voices amplified through megaphones. People were being directed to join queues, men were shouting and arguing, others were sounding distraught and over the top of it all they heard babies crying.

Before Henry could stop her, Leah had rushed outside. The sound of the babies on the radio followed her as she leapt over the picket fence and up the path, heading straight to the central bed of the Apricot Babes. She gathered their stems towards her bosom. They were perfect even beneath the heavy grey sky, their petals shone like prize winning medals. There she stayed as the layers of dust floated down from the sky.

The Mission

Gabriel watched Michael's tattoo strain with each movement, how the smile on the face of the Mona Lisa increased with the broadening bicep. Her lips were drawn up as if she was in a gurning contest. He almost forgot the discomfort of being pushed and twisted and stuffed into the safety harness. When he finally looked down, it seemed that now he had the waist of a twelve year old. As he climbed onto the platform his thoughts were taken up by the pressure on his testicles.

It occurred to him that if he was ever to have children it would not be because of fear of his own mortality. He had seen that in other people's eyes, beyond all the talk, and he understood what happened as people became older. They needed to have children. It was a life goal. These newborns were an extension of their own lives, a reseeding of the elements of their genes, a likeness of themselves, their habits, and if nothing else, a memory of their essence to be stored within the DNA to resurface in future generations. It was a roundabout way of becoming immortal.

All of this did not apply to Gabriel because he had no sense of having to fit so much into a decreasing life span. He had no sensibility that one day he would perish. Why would he? For as long as he could remember—and that was a very long time, people had always told him that he never seemed to age. So, he supposed, quite reasonably, that he would always remain that way.

Despite everything, he still cared for the betterment of those who existed today, particularly the young people. He cared a lot. In fact, he signed every petition going: Save the Nursery School from Demolition, the Seedlings Playgroup Petition for New Funds, The Junior League Football Pitch Drainage Scheme,

Anti Bully Week, Save the Mini Mobile Library of Books for Babies; anything that meant the children could have a better childhood. Lately, he had become anxious for the school leavers too; those who were leaving school without any qualifications, motivation or useable skills. In fact, it was for the youth of the town that he was doing this now. This would be his legacy.

"I think I need the toilet," he squeaked.

Michael shook his head to indicate he was not about to undo the harness under any circumstances.

"You've only just been, Gabe. Just hold your nerve. You know you can do it. I know you can do it."

"Ten."

The crowd was chanting and the great countdown had begun. Gabriel could feel their excitement, their anticipation. But the roar of their cries seemed all out of proportion. At that moment he couldn't be quite sure whether people genuinely wanted him to succeed or if the goodness of their hearts had given way to some more basic instinct. Perhaps they had reverted and they were baying for his blood, as if they were in the Coliseum of Ancient Rome. There were comparisons: he was being sent into the ring to battle against the odds, in this case, the elements, and become a hero or ... what?   Not exactly slaughtered, but there was always the possibility that he might fall to his death from a great height. Perhaps he was grossly exaggerating the task, but Gabriel did feel as though everyone was expecting something great, something momentous, to happen.

It would all be worth it in the end. After all, the church fete only brought in a measly couple of hundred pounds, the Rotary raffle even less, and the 10K run was a joke when it came to fund raising. It wasn't that there were not enough runners; just that no one could be bothered to find sponsors and then collect on the promises. This time it was different. So many tickets had been sold that every man, woman and child in the village must have shaken out their piggy banks, emptied their whisky bottle coppers, put the milk bill on hold, and bought as many tickets as they could. In return, each purchaser had stuck a pin into the county map and the corresponding location had been plotted in the form of coordinates.

Gabriel's fear was that he would get as far as the coast, some twenty five miles away, and become stuck on a cliff top. Worse still, he might drift out across the sea with the humiliation of being saved by an air sea rescue squad. He already had nightmares about helicopter blades slicing into the balloons and him plummeting hundreds of feet downwards into the ocean. He wasn't a great swimmer.

Michael had very sensibly predicted that he would only get as far as the little patch of land beyond the trees just where the meandering river turned so sharply as to almost form an island. That would be fine. He could walk home from there.

The local shopkeepers had been very generous with their donations. The winning ticket holder could: a) drink as much as they wanted at the Farmer's Arms for a night (and that included the lock-in), b) run a trolley around the supermarket in a mad dash to grab as much as they could in one minute, or, c) fill up with sweets from the corner shop. The youth fund would have all the money raised from the ticket sales. Job done.

"Nine!"

The balloons were jostling and shifting against each other. The stretching and straining of the ropes drew Gabriel's attention upwards and what he saw looked more like a great pink mattress and its buoyant enthusiasm reflected an almost divine effervescence. From within the tightly packed bunch came bird like tweets as each foil coated pillow brushed against the other.

Over and over they chattered, repeating the same sounds almost like an incantation derived from the words that were printed on them.

He dared not think about the nature of the materials; the fragile exteriors, the ethereal unpredictable fillings: such slight elements on which he was about to bestow his life. All he knew was that helium was non-flammable unlike, say, hydrogen. He had felt so much better when he found that out, not that he was a smoker or anything and he was unlikely to come across live flames in the sky apart from the outside possibility of fork lightning. He'd always hated fireworks.

When it came to helium versus body weight he was an expert. The internet was a good source of such useful facts and ways of calculating. There would certainly be enough balloons to lift him up from the ground. Exactly how far was less predictable because that would depend on other factors, ones that no one could control. Bets had been laid on things like height, angle, lift, duration of flight. Gabriel had been dieting for the past few weeks in preparation. In fact he'd lost almost a stone in weight since the original weigh-in. It was his secret. It would put pay to those know-it-all's who stroked their beards and theorised with the precision of a mathematical formula.

"Eight!"

Gabriel stood on the platform as if he was a little boy again at a school assembly; his knees pressed together, waiting for the bell to ring. His abiding memories of schooldays; pressing his knees together and never using the toilets. For one thing they stank and if he needed to sit on the seat it was always wet and sometimes they were even booby-trapped with extremely adhesive glue. There were other things that happened in the boys lavatories that he never wanted to think about again. His schooldays had not been happy, more of a dangerous game of avoidance at all costs. He'd studied the skills of self camouflage. He'd even had a whole summer holiday dressed entirely in pavement grey so that whenever he saw a group of children coming towards him down the street or in the park — it could be boys or girls— it made no difference to the slight of their malice — he would dive to the ground and roll away behind a bush or a bin and wait until they had passed by.

Most times he remained unnoticed but now was not one of them. He had truly put his head above the parapet. The crowd around him were getting rowdier and their shouts competed with the bells that were ringing out in glorious peels. His efforts had not gone unnoticed by the Reverend Allcroft who had mentioned Gabriel that very morning in his church service.

"A true angel of the people," he had declared and smiled benignly from the pulpit.

Gabriel had flushed to the roots of his brunette curls when the entire congregation turned around and beamed at him.

"Seven, Six!"

The chanting was gaining speed.

Now, he could hardly believe that he was going to allow himself to be lifted into the sky by a bunch of left over party balloons. What had seemed like a good idea and a fun way to raise funds for the youth scheme, all of a sudden felt like a ludicrous, and frankly, suicidal plan.

It had all started on his way home from choir practice one dismal evening when he passed two teenagers slunk in a shop doorway. It was raining. They were tipping small bottles of vodka into the cavity of their hoods, and from their hands came winding snakes of 'smoke'. One of them turned his back towards the entrance as Gabriel approached. All Gabriel could see was the back of a grey hoodie with an illustration of a dagger down its length. Then both lads turned around to face Gabriel and followed him with stony eyes.

He was determined not to be intimidated by them but as he walked past he felt intensely aware of the cut of his jacket. He liked to keep it buttoned up to the throat, he liked the perfect symmetry of the pockets and cuffs, he like the extra darts in the cut of the waist. But for all that he felt restricted as if his body was kept under control, as if there was something underneath crying out for escape. Michael was always telling him that he should relax more, loosen up. He'd even given him a kaftan for his birthday but Gabriel had never worn it. The idea of wearing tracksuit bottoms and hooded top was an enigma to him. He expected the two young men to fling out a comment like a provocative gauntlet; but in fact, they remained silent.

Once he'd passed further down the street, he reflected that their stance, rather than being threatening was actually one of hopelessness. They weren't unusual. These days there were so many young people who hung around the bus station, round the back of the shopping arcade, in the little park with the low fence, anywhere that gave them a space away from the rest of the population. If there was no possibility of finding work, of being useful in any way, simply because they were deemed to be children, then it was only reasonable that they should have somewhere to hang out. Gabriel mused on this idea. It had to be a place that was welcoming and comfortable, a place where they would feel safe, where they could begin to imagine new possibilities. It was at that moment that Gabriel decided to do something about it.

For years people had talked about opening a Milk Bar – at least a modern day version of one. Some thought it could be an extension to the youth club but whatever good ideas they had, they always failed. Nobody was really that bothered it seemed; they just wanted the youth to disappear and reappear once they had achieved maturity and the usual sensibilities of adulthood. People were not prepared to put their money into a scheme that might well be trashed, vandalised or covered in graffiti.

Gabriel knew that the first thing he had to do was to raise the money. It had to be something different. It was Michael who had come up with the idea. He worked at an elderly care home, one that prided itself on being a 'family' home. Michael could be quite cynical at times and claimed that it was all part of the marketing package. But whatever the motivation, it worked. There was a long waiting list of elderly folk wanting to make it their final residency.

One of the finer selling points was that birthdays and significant anniversaries were always celebrated in style. There had been such an occasion recently when the usual party paraphernalia was ordered for Elsie May Spiggot who had reached her one hundredth birthday. A bouquet of flowers was presented to the centigenarian along with a book of the highlights in verse and pictures of her life. Special napkins and mats for the table were bought and bunting and streamers retrieved from the cupboards. They even ordered one hundred pink balloons with the words, 'Elsie Mae's one hundred today!' and a cylinder of helium gas, but when the consignment of extra large pink balloons arrived, no one had bothered to check it until a few minutes before the auspicious event. That was when the extra nought had been discovered. Due to their personalised nature the excess balloons could not be sent back to the retailer or used on another occasion for another client.

"It would put the balloons to good use," Michael suggested as if it was the obvious thing to do with nine hundred left over balloons.

"Yes, that's all very well," Gabriel said, "but you know how I feel about heights."

Gabriel was incredulous. What could Michael possibly be thinking? He must know how Gabriel felt. They'd known each other long enough. Michael had always been the one to relish the chance of an abseil, a bungee jump, a freefall to a slow count of ten. There was something in his nature that made him want to fly but Gabriel was just not made like that. He preferred to have two feet on the ground. He actually liked gravity.

"Five!" yelled the crowd.

Perhaps, he thought, he was merely a spectator at a rocket launch, the final stages in the preparation for a new mission to send a man into space. Perhaps they weren't really looking at him at all but to some place beyond him, like at the industrial park where the mission had been kept secret until today. So what was he doing here? He looked over his shoulder and all around. No, there was no mistake. Everyone was definitely looking at him. He tried to believe that he was dreaming but the truth of his circumstance came back to him with brutal reality. He was strapped into a full body harness and about to be launched into the atmosphere and left to dangle from a mass of helium-filled pink decorations.

A single purpose built balloon with a firing cylinder with its own control mechanisms would have been infinitely more desirable. And then there was the wildcard factor of the weather. It had been decided (not by Gabriel, mind you) that the plan should go ahead whatever the weather, except in extreme circumstances. By that, they meant: tornado, hurricane, fork lightning— that kind of thing.

"Four!"

The wooden platform under Gabriel's feet shook and the strings above him began to tighten, reminding him of a hangman's gallows. He'd recently watched a programme about the gallows site at Tyburn in London where many executions had taken place in olden times. What had really stayed with him was how the population had treated it like a carnival. Shops and workplaces shut, even apprentices were given time off and it was just like a modern public holiday. All the family would come out to watch the latest hanging.

Gabriel looked out across the crowd. He could see parents with children, babies in buggies, grandparents. Some had come with camping chairs or those walking sticks where the top unfolds out into a little perch. They were all smiling up at him, trustingly, expectantly, and somehow he felt that if he showed any sign of weakness they might just begin to jeer at him. He looked up at the balloons. How had this ever seemed like a good idea?

"Three!"

Now the back of the brace began to tighten along the hollows on either side of his spine. It was fortunate that it fitted snugly enough between his shoulder blades avoiding the sore patches. There had been many practice runs, jumps and simulated flights at the aerodrome. Michael, who had once embarked on his pilot training but never completed it, had gone with him. They had borrowed a glider from a retired Air Force major who'd been very enthusiastic about the project and had even offered to teach him himself when he'd heard about Gabriel's vertigo.

"I'll show him a thing or two about height," he'd declared. "He'll soon get over that!"

Michael declined the offer.

"We'll manage," he'd said firmly. "Very kind of you to offer."

At first, they sat in the cockpit while Michael talked him through the controls. When Gabriel took hold of the control stick, he put his foot on the rudder, closed his eyes and imagined that he was up there, cruising along a cusp of a cloud. But then a crow landed on the glider's wing and startled him. Gabriel believed that he would drop to the ground forgetting that he had not even left it in the first place and in a panic had scrambled and fumbled until he had found a way out. That was when he scraped his back along the hatch. The wound had never quite healed.

"Two!"

The main rope was clipped to his harness. Michael tugged at the karabiner and again at the one over Gabriel's head. His life now depended on two D-shaped metal rings.

"All nice and tight," Michael declared. "Are we ready?"

The question echoed in Gabriel's mind. He knew that there was no 'we' about it.

"You coming too then, Mike?" he quipped.

Michael ignored him, giving the ropes a sharp double tug.

"One!" the crowd shouted.

Gabriel was on his own now. He could see across the park to where the teenagers were kicking a can against the doors of the changing rooms. Before Gabriel could say anything more the crowd roared.

"Blast off!" they all screamed.

The balloons were released from the block that secured them and Gabriel felt them pulling. It wasn't a bad sensation; it was like being gently stretched. He had always supposed that he would ascend with a jolt but it was a long time before his feet were level with the shoulders of the adults. Anyone could have raised a hand and pulled him back down. It was a comforting thought – but nobody did. He looked at Michael who was standing the centre of the crowd; his head was tilted upwards, his eyes closed and his hands pressed together. As Gabriel followed the line of his gaze he thought he saw a flicker of light from above. A flash of lightning. This could be his get out clause. It wasn't too late. But no one else seemed to have noticed and it did not happen again.

The crowd cheered.

Perhaps it was really quite an easy way to raise money after all and then there was the bonus of becoming a local hero.

He kicked his feet out and flapped his arms.

"I'm flying," he called.

He was soon lifted way above the heads of the crowd and as he rose, the world became smaller; the green of the park was soon the size of a napkin within the rows of toy houses. He drifted for a while; his flight was more of a leisurely, slow, gentle cruise. He did not experience the sudden rush of vertigo that he had imagined in all the weeks of preparation. It could even be a little more exciting than this he thought. He looked up at the balloons. They seemed secure and oddly enough, they looked happy, if it was possible to extrapolate such feelings from a bunch of balloons. They were, after all, going to be his friends.

He soon reached a level where he no longer rose. He thought it must be the height of optimum elevation for this mode of transport. He could see a tree ahead of him and in order to rise a little more and not to crop the green crest of leaves, he pulled on the ropes, tucked his legs up under him, closed his eyes and made ready to float over the top.

"Come on Elsie Mae," he called.

There was a crinkling sound and it was a moment before he dared to look up. Some of the balloons had shrivelled and he shivered as he looked back down. It was an awful long way and dotted amongst the trees were several outcrops of rock.

"Help!" he screamed.

There was no one to hear him. Those who had been following him from the ground had been cut off by the river and the woods. There were more trees ahead.

Pop.

Gabriel felt the lessening hold of the balloons. All around him in the tree tops were spherical weavings of twigs. Nests. From his vantage point he could look straight into the open beaks of the baby rooks. There was something endearing and cute and vulnerable about them and in some ways they reminded Gabriel of the youngsters who really were still fledglings unable to escape the home base.

Pop, pop, pop.

There it was again. The sound seemed to agitate the adult birds and they began to fly out from the nest, circling. The popping became incessant and Gabriel realised that they were deliberately bursting the balloons.

"Hey, what do you think you're doing?" he exclaimed.

"Stop it! Stop it, right now!"

He realised the seriousness of his situation. His calls were muffled as he was struck across the face by a black wing. He flailed around and batted at it, striking it with his hand, sending it into a spasm of fury. It soon regained its perch on his shoulder and batted his face with a flurry of stiff feathers.

"Help!" he called.

Then more were coming towards him. Surely they could see that he was no threat. It was at that point that he realised that the birds were attracted to the shiny objects above his head and that as their beaks struck into the soft foil he was beginning to descend.

The birds continued carking and flocking until Gabriel was surrounded by more black than pink. The edges of the harness were hurting too and the sores on his back felt hot and raw. He broke out into a sweat and lifted his arms to allow the cool air to flow into his armpits. He was now surrounded by more birds, squawking and pecking at him. He thrashed around pulling at the harness but even in his state of panic he knew that it would be foolish to unclip the ropes. In any case something was still holding him up. The balloons must be made of sturdier stuff than he realised or perhaps their incessant chattering had invoked the spirit of Elsie Mae. It was a fanciful thought but he held on to it for a moment, imagining that she was stretching out a helping hand from the heavens.

Then he noticed that not all of the feathers around him were black. The ones below his arms were white and fine but definitely fully matured judging by the shape of their quills. And then, to add to his surprise, he realised they were part of a structured wing. As he lifted his shoulders in the effort to see them more clearly, they moved. His shirt was bulging and the seams were stretched taut. He could see the stitching giving way until it finally split open. The buttonholes acted as catapults, releasing the buttons all around. The curious birds flew away, circling downwards, attracted by the tiny shiny discs. Finally with shirt was completely split at the seams and the pieces of material floated to the ground.

His wings were freed. Without a second thought he unclipped the karabiners, detached the ropes and unbuckled the harness. He hovered for a moment as he watched the flaccid pink balloons drifting away and down towards the ground. He watched as the ropes hit the turf just within the curve of the river, at the place that Michael had predicted. He felt released at last. His body was no longer encased; he was a free spirit, liberated from his earthly form, not floating with the aid of a few hundred balloons but actually flying, flying high above the trees, up and up into the endless space of the sky. The whole world lay below him and it was his, all his. He could go wherever he wanted, do whatever he pleased. He felt strangely empowered.

He stretched out his new wings; diving earthwards, circling, rising up, diving down again and headed back towards the town. He swept back along the deserted main street. The shops had closed as people were either at the park awaiting news of his landing or they had given up and gone home when they had lost sight of him.

He stopped by the doorway of the closed up shop, the one that he had passed on that dismal day. He thought there was no one there at first but then he noticed the bundles in the corner. As his eyes adjusted to the light he realised that there were three or four youngsters crouched in the back of the entrance. They were passing something around and had a large-eyed look of wonderment. The biggest lad stood up when Gabriel's shadow fell over them. In two strides he bounded towards him but not in the way of an attack but more like a gleeful spaniel.

"Wow," he called back to his mates. "Take a look at this."

The others came to the entrance and gawped at Gabriel.

"Crazy, man!"

"Are you for real, mister?" one of them asked.

He was young and looked a little afraid as Gabriel fluttered his wings.

"It's just me," he said. "Gabriel. Only I've got wings now."

Even Gabriel had to check over his back, just to be sure.

"Can you get us some of those too?" the smaller one asked.

"I don't see why not," Gabriel replied. "It seems that anything's possible."

The Inventions of Mr Pitikus

The wind blew all the time; it was a fact. Plants and trees grew horizontal to the ground. In summer the soil was scorched by the sun and the sand storms wrecked the island with spasmodic twister winds that ripped through the earth. In winter everything became elongated, not just the hours of darkness but the sound of the unremitting race of the wind. Icicles stuck out sideways from fence posts and became long shards of glass often to the misfortune of the birds that flew into them and remained there pierced through the heart. A cow had escaped from a shed and within a few hours it was pinned against an iron fence; it's ripped flesh flaunted by the wind.

The people of Windblatter built their houses so that the roofs bowed down to the ground on the windward side. The only daylight filtered in through the narrow slit windows on the lee. Each house had metal bonded ropes thrown over them and pegged into the ground and fixed there with an aggregate of granite and burnt lime. Fireplaces were boarded over in the winter when the winds were at their strongest because there was little point in lighting a fire when immediately it would be sucked up and away through the chimney. Rooms became burrows as people dug further into the ground where the temperature was constant.

For food, they mainly existed on the mushrooms that grew in their cellars along with a little meat and milk that they exchanged for their wares. Once a month each family would pack up their cart with woven cloth, hammered metal pans, handmade clay pots or whatever it was that they produced; each house had a speciality. It took three men or more to drag the cart to the Great Barn where all of their mercantile transactions were performed at the Trading Post. In winter the men could be seen in the streets wrapped in white scarves that went around their bodies, necks and heads. They looked like zombies with their stiff, stooped demeanour. Such precautions were necessary to stop the acid effect of the wind as too much exposure would blind them.

By fermenting their excess mushrooms they found they could produce liquor that was stronger than any of the whiskey that floated ashore from the wrecks. They cursed many a ship for successfully negotiating the rocks in the storms; their rich pickings sailing by just out of reach. The long winter nights were spent supping their mushroom wine after putting a drop or two in the children's bedtime drinks. It helped the little ones to sleep through the dreary hours where the constancy of the whistling wind filled their sleep with nightmares. For the adults, it was easy to overdo the drink and the wine had an uncanny effect of causing hallucinations of the fantastical kind that meant they were reluctant to return to the daytime world of Windblatter. Understandably, they would have preferred to continue with their dream lives of other more comfortable places.

Rollo Pitikus was different. He was not a drinker; he was an inventor who worked day and night on his creations. He kept himself to himself, which was just as well. He could never hold a normal conversation or respond in an appropriate manner. When the kindly souls from the WIC (Windblatter Institute of Cakery) called by with their Pat-a-Cakes, he waved them away.

"There's no time for that kind of thing here," he'd say. "I've work to do..."

Even in the summertime when people were darting between the houses, calling in here and there for the Gossipings he had no interest in the ins and outs of their everyday lives. He was only concerned with the minutiae of the turbines, cogs and rotators that made up his latest invention: the Great Stilling Machine. Seven years of his life had been spent trying to find a way to stop the wind but as with so many of his gadgets and devices it had, so far, resulted in failure. His idea was to make a machine that could suck in the air using its own energy and push it back out again — the same air without the energy. In other words, it would produce still air without the movement of wind. It was not a concept that anyone else could really get their heads around as it seemed unimaginable that air could be anything other than the swift streams that relentlessly billowed around the island.

Now it was springtime and the dark wintering was over. People were beginning to emerge from their homes and hideouts. Mr Pitikus had made twenty five machines and he was keen to try them out. The idea was to spread them in a line across the island, switch them on simultaneously and wait for the result. He had worked out the precise coordinates where each machine should be placed. There were many factors to take into consideration: the geography of the land, soil erosion, the angle of the sun. It was vital there should be no mistakes. He needed the help of the islanders and he knew that now was the right moment to engage them. Emerging from their winter hallucinatory states they could be persuaded to do almost anything even to take part in one of his madcap schemes.

It took four strong people to move each machine; they were that heavy. The furthest they would have to go was five miles and that was over land covered with the meshed clumps of the indigenous Vertiginous Grass with its sword-like blades that could cut a man's foot straight from the ankle. It took many days of hard labour and several returned home with nasty injuries.

Meanwhile, the others who had stayed at home had grown into the spirit of the exercise and had set about making food for an opening ceremony: Chooley pies, Haw Berry Tarts and the famous Windblatter Warble Cake with its iced wind tunnels and candle funnels. They had even made streamers, bunting and chimes; things that they would not normally contemplate. This time they had put their faith in Mr Pitikus's invention but perhaps it was just an overabundance of hope and optimism.

Eventually, everything was in place and a young member of the community was invited to switch on the machines. One flick of a central lever would initiate the starting mechanisms of all the other machines. The community gathered around, wrapped up as usual in their cloths and bindings. Behind each mask was a pair of curious eyes focussed on the other side of the island. There was no grand speech, no declaration; there would not be any point, as a single voice would be whipped away before it could be heard.

Mr Pitikus signalled to the child. The switch was flicked and the great turbines began to churn. Everyone watched as the blades rotated faster and faster and they felt the suck of the machines pulling at the wind. Somebody's head gear flew off and momentarily the machines stopped but after a grinding and a whiff of burning they carried on.

Nothing changed for the first fifteen minutes and people were beginning to feel a familiar sense of disappointment.

But then it happened.

Some of them stumbled, tripped and fell onto their backsides as the air was stilled. They looked around at the trees and plants whose tops usually brushed the ground and saw that they were beginning to spring up. People looked at each other and began to speak, amazed that they could hear each others' words without the wind turning their voices into an ululation. Slowly, they unloaded their carts of tables, chairs, food and drink and the party began. They waved their cloths around, throwing them up into the sky and watching with astonishment as they drifted back down to their feet. They danced and hugged and ate and drank.

The celebration went on for several days until a youngster, in a state of delusion, ran back into the wind side, surfing and whooping and diving until a current of air carried him into the jaws of the turbines. There was a ripple of shock through the gathering as they all stared at the wall of empty air before them where only minutes ago the boy had scrambled against the force, half in fear, half in exhilaration. The elders gave out stern warnings to all the other young people.

It was not long before one bright spark had a realisation: if they could have half the island back then why not have the whole? A delegation was formed and they went to see Mr Pitikus, who by then was a crowned hero. They asked if they could move the machines over to the edge of the coast so that the whole of the island could enjoy the perfect wind free climate.

Pitikus was slightly the worse for wear with an overdose of mushroom wine; in fact, in his mind he was on a tropical island with beautiful girl servants bringing him sweet Jaduboo fruits, the milk of the Coshola and anything else he desired. His great scientific brain had gone soft and slippery and he no longer felt his customary grumpiness. He smiled and gurgled in agreement. Waving a regal hand he said,

"You carry on, my work is done. Now is the time to rest and play."

So they organised themselves into gangs in order to shift each of the Wind Stillers, as the machines were now called. They agreed to do it simultaneously without switching them off so that their partying comrades would not be disturbed. The idea was to reposition the machines at the far edges of the island.

They were careful to make sure that each appliance was exactly the same number of crow meters apart and at the same altitude as the first positions worked out by Mr Pitikus. They could not risk any runaway wind breakers thwarting the procedure so they checked and rechecked their measurements before heaving the Wind Stillers into their new locations. It was hard labour and took a dozen men to move each machine. They worked together, shouting their instructions along a line that stretched the girth of the island. The result was exactly as they had hoped: the entire island became bathed in a warm windless light.

Unfortunately, just as they were enjoying the fruits of their labours it began to rain. It came in little spots at first and no one took any notice. But then the rain got heavier and heavier. The people looked up to the sky. They were puzzled. There were no grey clouds so where did the rain come from? And why did it have to rain on the first day of their lives when they could all be together enjoying themselves out of doors?

Rollo Pitikus lay on a bed of Pallumo leaves, his belly stuffed full of good food and every now and then he lifted a bottle to his mouth before falling back into a fabulous dreamy doze. He licked his lips as the rain fell. Even the sky was praising him now with droplets of wine, or was it the tears of the flummoxed wind? It did taste rather salty after all. The rain fell faster and Mr Pitikus slept on but in his sleep his brain began to reform and then a buzz of puzzlement ran through it. He sat up and looked over to his machines, or at least to where his machines were earlier that day or was it the day before? He was not used to feeling the fuzzy after affects of the mushroom liquor and he began to panic.

"Where are my Machines?" he asked in a quavering voice.

"No worries, Mr Pitikus." The young man who spoke looked up at him from an open bowl. His chin was dribbling with seeds of the Cherisha. Mr Pitikus looked at the bowls of empty cocktails surrounding him and groaned.

"Everything's worked out just fine, Mr Pitikus sir," the man grinned and continued lapping the golden liquid.

"Oh no! What have you done? My machines; where are they?"

Rollo Pitikus was on his feet and looking all around him now.

"We moved them to the edges of the island just as you agreed."

But it was all too late. By the time he reached them, they could not be turned off. The salt water had rusted the main lever and all the other switches. By now the island was an inch deep in the sea water that had been sucked into the machines and out the other side. Faster and faster the milled water flooded around them. The energy the water produced was even greater than that of the wind and soon the streets were filled with floating furniture. Windows were falling in with the pressure of the rising water

There was only one place left for them to go and that was the Great Barn which fortunately had been built on a piece of raised land. Every man, woman and child gathered in the barn. They bolted the doors and climbed up the ladders to the upper level but soon the waters were beginning to seep between the floor boards.

"We must cut the ropes," Pitikus declared.

They began to argue with each other. For years the ropes had been their lifelines and now they were being asked to sever their cords. They could not see the sense in it.

"If it had not been for your stupid machines we would not be in this mess now," one woman declared. They all turned towards him as he protested.

"It was because you moved them," he shouted.

41

He jumped onto a pile of boxes behind him to escape their jeers and clawing hands.

"Look, the island is disappearing into the sea. We will all perish if we do not act now."

A sudden rush of water swept through their legs and stopped them in their stride.

"Loosen the ropes," he shouted, "Let's hope the barn is strong enough to float."

The mushroom wine was starting to wear off now and people were looking tired and scared and they could see that there was no other choice. By now the whole barn was creaking and pulling at the guy ropes. It was obvious that if they stayed tethered, the barn would break up and float away in bits and boards and they would all drown. They grabbed the saw blades that hung on the high hooks and with the sharpest blades they cut through the ropes.

The Great Barn began to rise up and tilt from side to side as each rope was severed. Everyone screamed and shouted. Then, all of a sudden they were upright, bobbing along on a calm and breezeless sea. In the background they could hear the gurgling sound as the rotating machines disturbed the deep waters under the ocean.

They floated along for days and nights until they could no longer tell how far they were from the island. The rock they called their home had completely disappeared. Now and again a stray wave tilted the barn and everyone fell against each other as they hit the side. Eventually a brave girl volunteered to be the look out and she scrambled up onto the roof. She shouted whenever a roller was coming towards them.

'Wave A Hoy.'

The Windblatter folk held tightly on to each other as the shouts become more and more frequent. Finally, one huge wave shoved them up so high that they could no longer see the sea below. Up and up they went. There seemed to be no end to this wave. It was as if they were travelling towards the summer moon until they were held in a cusp of cloud within a pale blue sky. Around them, the air was so still that their breath made no impact. The children blew into each other's faces as hard as they could but not a hair moved. There were no waves, no sudden jolts, just calmness all around them. And under the ocean the inventions of Mr Pitikus churned on and on.

Bugs

The wall had begun to crumble, not because of the attention that Katy was giving it but because of the intense heat. As she swung her legs, her heels clunked against the brickwork sending a powdery red dust into the air. A bee disappeared into a crevice in the wall and as she waited for it to reappear, Uncle Cedric arrived.

He waved at her and gave an exaggerated grin from behind the steering wheel, but all Katy noticed were the damp underarms of his shirt. Aunty Vi had a green tinged pallor and the reason for this only became apparent when the car door was opened. It was not the smell of sweat that overpowered the sweet scents of the flowering japonica; it was the aroma of urine.

"It's all right for you," Aunty Vi was saying to Uncle Cedric as she pulled herself out of the passenger seat. "You can't smell a thing since you had that op on your polyps."

Katy peered into the back. Great Aunty Shula was asleep, slumped sideways, her mouth twisted open; her breath had steamed up the quarter light.

Aunty Vi gave Katy a hug.

"For you," she said handing her a large jar. It was a sweet jar, the kind that filled the shelves at Parker's newsagents, but this one was not full to the brim with brightly coloured gobstoppers, pink sherbets, chocolate limes or liquorice sticks. It was more like a miniature garden inside a greenhouse, an untended forest of leaves and twigs, and it was secured with string around a piece of net that formed the lid.

"Giant Stick Insects!" Aunty Vi said and she winked.

Katy peered into the jungle.

"Ah, there you are!" Mother said, appearing beside them. "What took you so long?"

"Cedric had to go to the garage to collect the car," Vi told her. "Those cheap tyres dissolved within a week and a hose needed replacing. Everything's melting in this heat. You can see the tar running off the roads."

"It's shocking, absolutely shocking," Mother said. "I don't know why they can't do something about it."

"...and then by the time we collected Aunty, well ..."

They were now entering the house.

The tea had already been laid out. There were plates of ham, sausage rolls, bowls of crisps, and slices of tomatoes cut with zigzag edges. Everything sweated under drum tight plastic.

Mother led Aunty Shula to the upright armchair, the one with the throw. Then she hugged her sister, Vi. Katy could see her mother's face over her aunt's shoulder and the ensuing grimace. For a moment her mother's lips remained frozen in a pucker, her gaze petrified, fixed on the table. Next to the breadsticks, where Katy had place it, was the jar; the one with the stick insects.

"What on earth!" Mother exclaimed but before she could move Katy had grabbed it and run outside. The new car was warm and glowed invitingly in the sunlight. As she pulled out the leaves, the insects sprung out and she watched them as they disappeared between the cracks along the edges of the bonnet.

When she went back to the living room the kerfuffle had died down and Father was greeting Cedric with a formal hand shake. They embarked on their usual conversation regarding the route that Cedric had taken to get from his house to theirs. The new car had made the journey so much easier.

"Got it for a good price too," Cedric explained. "'Course, they know me there."

He tapped the side of his nose.

Katy withdrew to her favourite place behind the sofa

where she had hidden the gold lining papers from a cigarette carton. She began to make her goblet but she was still able to watch the others via the mirror over the fireplace.

"Don't be too cross with her," Aunty Vi was saying to Mother. "You should count your blessings."

Vi and Cedric had not had children and Katy had heard her mother saying how very sad that must be for them. Katy was sad too. She would have liked to have had some cousins to play with.

"It's all very well but she has the most annoying habits," Mother said. Her eyes narrowed. "I'm sure she does it on purpose. We try our very best."

"Did you hear we've got a new puppy?" Vi announced loudly. "It's a rescue. The poor thing has had such a hard time. Lovely temperament though."

"I don't know how you put up with all those animals." Mother shivered.

"What is it now? Two dogs, three cats, a chinchilla..."

"Don't forget the hens," Vi added. "I love the little noises they make when they bustle around," and she demonstrated by making soft clucking sounds.

"Maybe next time you should marry a farmer," Mother blushed.

"I'll pop me clogs soon enough don't you worry," Cedric said, turning to Father.

"Drives me potty at times, she does," he continued, "house like a menagerie. Home's not your own."

Father made no reply.

"So, how's Katy getting on at the new school?" Vi asked Mother.

Katy saw her mother's eyebrows lifting.

"Well, I told them that they won't get a peep from her."

Her voice lowered to a whisper.

"She never even laughs. It's not normal."

She mouthed the word 'normal', but Katy could read lips, even those reflected in a mirror. As she pulled her index finger out of the golden bowl of the cup, Katy began to smooth the edges of the rim. It would make a fine champion's cup.

"Have you thought about getting her a pet?" Aunty Vi asked. "They say it can really help."

"I won't have animals in this house, think of the germs!" Mother said. "It's bad enough that she plays with worms and woodlice and God knows what. I don't know how she can bear to touch those things."

Vi was quiet.

"Did you see the news last night?" Mother continued. "Because of the heat wave there are swarms of flying beetles all along the coast."

She shivered.

"Tropical bugs related to scorpions!"

Mother was apparently unable to sit still so she went off into the kitchen. By now, the lounge was sweltering. The French doors had remained firmly shut and there were little droplets of moisture forming under the plastic sheeting that covered most of the carpet.

All was quiet for a moment until the door from the kitchen burst open. Mother was pushing a trolley that clattered and rattled with cups and saucers. Her face was red and she looked flustered.

"I can't be doing with this heat!" she exclaimed.

She poured out the tea and handed around a plate of biscuits.

"Katy, stop hiding!" She placed the cup of orange squash and a currant biscuit onto the smallest nest table. "I know you're there." Her voice was sharp.

Katy twisted the stem of the goblet as tight as she could. Then she reached out for a currant biscuit and began to pick out the 'flies'.

Great Aunty Shula was settled into the armchair with a glass ashtray balanced on the arm. She seemed oblivious to her gathered family. Her guppy mouth opened and closed as the smoke rings rose, drifting up towards the ceiling.

"I know I shouldn't but nothing seems to work," Cedric was saying, taking another cigarette from the packet.

"Anyway you only need to look at Bert up the road," he said, with the cigarette between his lips.

He continued talking but to Katy he sounded just like the ventriloquist on the TV, the one with the dummy with scary eyes.

"Ninety two and smoked since he was a nipper."

"It's not done him much harm," Father agreed.

Katy's goblet was nearly finished now. Only the bottom needed to be splayed out and then she would have a perfect trophy for her worm races.

"'Course, I could always try hypnotherapy?" Cedric said but he did not sound as if he meant it.

"Load of old witchcraft!" Great Aunty Shula cackled into life.

Her voice spluttered and cracked until the phlegm caught in her throat and sent her into a fit of coughing. She waved away Aunty Vi's attempt to pat her back. Once the coughing had subsided, she sucked on her cigarette with increased vigour but before she could speak a shadow passed over them.

Mother was stood in the middle of the room, one arm held aloft, a rolled up magazine in her hand. Both men stood up simultaneously causing the sofa to tip back.

Slap!

She had struck the window pane. They all stared at the black and red smear on the glass. Katy was out through the French doors before anyone could stop her, leaving the golden goblet squashed under the sofa.

From the far corner of the garden she heard the others coming out. They stopped by the fence to look at the neighbour's hedge of burgeoning privet.

Katy had not noticed Aunty Vi approaching until she was right next to her.

"Take a look inside," Aunty Vi said, offering her a yellow matchbox.

Katy had to push quite hard to slide open the drawer. Inside, the safety matches had been replaced with a leaf and under it was what, at first, looked like a brooch but she soon realised that that was not the case. Two antennae waved up at her. It was a beautiful petrol blue beetle with yellow stripes along its sides. The metallic sheen caught in the sunlight as it lifted its wings. Katy smiled and gently closed the box.

Aunty Vi returned to the others who were beginning to make their way inside. Only Cedric remained in the garden. He had a gas lighter in one hand and his other hand was cupped around his mouth. Katy could see the flint of the lighter switching over and over; its spark dying each time.

"Bug..ga!" he exclaimed and was startled by Katy.

"'Scuse my French," he mumbled.

Katy held up the matchbox.

"Oh, thanks Katy," he said. "You're a good girl."

As he struggled to open the drawer, Katy's teeth pressed firmly into her lower lip.

"What the...?"

Cedric had dropped the box onto the ground. His face held an expression of terror as the beetle crawled over his shoe and tucked itself under the leather tongue. He jumped up and down violently stamping his foot, over and over. Then he shook one leg at a time with such force that Katy thought they might fall off.

She was shaking too, but not with fear. A loud guffaw exploded from her mouth as she laughed and laughed and laughed.

The Drowning

The husks jostle, scratching your palms. You don't know how they got there or where they came from. There are so many of them that you can hardly bear to look—their pale oval shells are like hatching insects vying for space. Finally there are just a couple left, sticking to your hand, clinging like static. You flick your fingers until the grains fall into the open sack. You look away and try not to think of about them. You know that if you do, you will be sucked into the dark depths, suffocated.

The lids of your eyes waver and open and when the filmy blur clears you see that the world is all white; the walls, the curtains around the bed, the bedcovers. You are in a shroud of white linen, cotton wool floats in clouds before your eyes.

You remember the whitewash; lifting the wide brush from the tin, slashing with careless strokes across the outer walls; how the brush filled the cracks, covering the stonework, leaving a soft powdering of white rock and how it came away on your clothes for ages afterwards whenever you brushed against it, marking you with white bruises. And the cottage; the cottage by the sea, is as close as a dwelling can be to the water. Tucked behind the rim of a dune, it is only yards from the reaching fingers of the upper line of the tide. You always went there, every summer throughout your childhood.

When your Father was alive, the family would drive to the coast; arrive, tumbling from the back door of the estate car, tipping out with buckets, spades, jelly sandals, windbreaks, mallets, picnic basket, a flask of tea 'for the journey'. Very soon the scent of the salt sea and sand has permeated your hair, your clothes, filled your lungs. With your siblings you compete – 'last to the sea is a silly twit' – and the shock of cold water crashes over your feet, your legs, your body, washing over your shoulders, your back, the gasp as you come up as if you have hit a sprung coil on the seabed. Wave after wave after wave follows you, chasing you back to the shore, dragging you into the maw. It is a struggle to get back up the shingle to the shoreline and there you let the warm shallows lap over you.

That was before the fatal day when Father was lured away, enticed by a shoal of mackerel. They were out in the bay, flaunting their petrol hides, gilt with sunbeams. Before the drowning, he spent his days perched on the corner stone of the wall, smoking his pipe, brooding, willing the ocean to keep its distance, watching for every hint of when the tide would turn; daring at its boldness. It had never yet breeched the wall. It would only take a couple of plucky waves on a stormy day to fill the well of the cobbled courtyard for the whole place to be swallowed, washed clean with brine. But in the old days they knew a thing or two about walls and tides and oceans. And so the cottage had remained dry for three centuries and the sea had always kept its bargain, staying to its own side of the tide line. But there was a price to pay, a sacrifice to be made.

The house had been your family's home for generations, part of the community of the fisher folk of Pontreith. They had lived amongst the cluster of families who had dwelled there for centuries, taking their fill from the sea, occasionally paying it back by losing a life to the ocean. If you stand below the graveyard on the cliff top and look down you will find the bones that have been thrown clear of the tide, cleansed over and over by the action of the salt wash, bleached by the sea. Too many young men have fallen overboard, caught by their own nets on a night of a rough sea. And in the Seaman's Mission, there is a chapel with an altar to those who never returned, believed to be lost, never found; their waving hands became mere tendrils to flail and flutter in the memory.

Your breathing is slow as you lift your hand but your arm is constrained by a line that is attached to a drip. You watch the slow movement of liquid sliding along the tube, pumping through your veins and arteries and you wonder how pure is the saline or whether its density is that of the sea. The tidal rhythm of the pulse in your neck is thudding the pillow, booming, sonic. You shift as far as you can down the bed until your face is covered by the sheet. The warm air below the surface lulls you back, into the dream where you are reaching for the coarse cloth of the sack, the sack full of grain. You gather it in, tie the neck with a loose thread of hessian, lift its weight and throw it over your back.

A road is unfolding from the mist in front of you and your feet step in and out of the rhyming words that are scrawled below you; their end words fall in dual metres. Step left and you hear an echo of the right and left again until the weight on your chest and legs becomes heavy. You ache, your breathing is shallow. You fight with all your strength and when the ground begins to rise, you rise with it as if lifted by a breeze. With your heart racing the wind, you push on and on until in the distance you see the horizon, a single line. You know it is the pale blue rope, the one that is stretched just above the ocean and below the sky, where the waves and water intermingle, placed there to catch those who might fall over the edge.

You'd gone back to the village. In recent years, the cottage has been used as a holiday let but times have changed and when few can afford a holiday it remains empty, its echoing voices turned inward, maligning, imprisoned within their whitewashed walls.

It was the only place you could go. After all, it is the place of your ancestors, the fields, the land, the coast that for so long gave succour to your people. The inland towns were flooded with water that fell from the sky, relentless rain, fresh, unsalted but just as capable of drowning. Rivers swelled, burgeoning, breaking their banks; great reservoirs of water formed in places where no lake had ever been before. Some were swept along in the wake, marooned on islands, clinging to a single tree. There were no bridges left and in the valleys the villages were left to gurgle under the great lagoons.

Some had run to the hills only to find that hundreds, sometimes thousands had had the same idea and when they arrived there was nothing for them, just many others. The trees had been felled for their firewood, saplings formed into benders to shelter far too many, bushes of berries had been razed by the hungry and the dark caves sparked with the fires that roasted the scarce remains of rabbits and rats, of cats and dogs.

And all you kept thinking about was how you must get to the cottage by the sea. You longed to wrap those thick walls around you, to graze the pantry packed with salted fish. If the world was filling with water then a sturdy cottage that was built to withstand the waves would be the safest place. Even the mullioned windows were angled towards the east so as not to let in the westerly forces of the weather. It had been a safe place for your ancestors, why should it not be for you? And if it came to the worst, you would fix up the old fishing boat, patch up the holes, tar the hull and sail off the anchor. You would be a modern day Noah—without the animals.

You never made it did you?

After a mile of walking under the weight of grain, you see a man at the edge of the dusty road. He sits with his legs crossed and looks as though he waits, staring straight ahead, his eyes ghosted with time, watching but not seeing. At his side is a basket; it is woven from sea grass, plucked from the swards along the salt shore line. As you stop in front of him he does not look up, does not flinch. It is as if your very shadow has no depth.

Inside the basket are many shells, the crusts of homes that were once dwelled in by the creatures of the sea, clinging to the rock pools or the overhanging edges of the cliffs. Urchins, cockles, winkles, razor shells, limpets with tiny barnacles still attached, and, a single starfish that is so dry as if it has succumbed to a sudden outburst of the sun, dried in a spasm, white, brittle, exposing its suckers.

The man holds out a hand, opening, closing, exposing his palm. You are surprised. It is a young hand, not gnarled or twisted with age but as it unfolds you see that it has no lines of fate or fortune, not even the crease of a heart. The fingertips have no prints and you wonder how he has survived with no identity; no past, no vision of a future and presumably, no hope. You are tempted by the shells and you ask him how much they are. You will pay him handsomely. He nods at you and holds up the basket as if to say, 'Take them all, they are yours to take.' But you say you cannot do that, he is too kind. But you will exchange a handful of grains for a single shell.

And so, into his lap you pour the wheat and take the starfish. But when you look at it there is something that you had not noticed before, something familiar. It is a hand of flesh with five splayed fingers. It is the hand that caught hold of you when the wave tilted and tipped the boat onto its side, capsizing, discharging you into the water. It is the hand that tightened around your arm, dragging and pulling you up from the sea bed until you could reach up and catch hold of the rim above the hull of the boat. You lay on the deck for a long while with sea water issuing from you.

You remember nothing more. You are here now, in a hospital, and you know that the sea has already staked a claim, before long it will come back for you. Your hands clasp together beneath the bed clothes, two starfish embracing. The incessant rain is drilling at the window; its beating is arrhythmic. You try to make sense of it, to draw it into a melody. And then you realise that it is calling your name. Three syllables at a time. You will not answer. You close your lips, folding them tight around your teeth. The pillow is falling over your head. You are engulfed in the haze of your own breath. Even your sweat no longer keeps you cool.

The light is muffled into a dark orange glow, as if the sun has yet to set. There is no shade, no well to drink from as you watch the flames, burning, burning. You see that they are coming from the dragons' mouths as they travel across the desert plains towards the night caves. They are crossing the veined land beneath the lids of your eyes. As they pass, their fire licks the dry tops of the corn in the fields, catching alight. You call out to the rain, the rain that beats so close, to come near enough to quench the fire. It cannot hear you; you cannot make it listen. Your forehead is heavy, a wet trickle reaches your ear and you look up and there you see the hand, the starfish hand. It is pressing down on your head, pushing you below, and all you hear are the waves.

The land is coming into sight now, although you are still at sea and you look towards the cliffs, the rolling land to where there is a house. You see through the window. On the kitchen table is a freshly baked loaf. It is a kitchen that you recognise and here is your grandmother, smiling, singing a line from a song, over and over. You join in but although she smiles she cannot hear you, she cannot see you. A yeasty aroma is filling the air, and the oven door with its spiral handles has been left open, the tops of the hot plates catch the light from the window. There is a bowl on the table too. It looks handmade from clay and in it is salt, rough sea salt. You hold the crystals between your fingers and they are brittle. As they crunch, they cut your skin.

Now the house is filled with the scent of the sea and as it rises, each room is bursting; the walls are cracking, the windows are flung from their catches, the white curtains are billowing, flapping across your face, your mouth, your nose. You catch your breath in shallows. The floors swell up with the pressure of the water beneath them until they burst through and you are lifted right off your feet. Now you are drawn towards the door, but as you grab the edge of the frame your fingers slip and you have no choice but to slip through the opening. You are pulled this way and that, down a path, through woods, along a road where you see the man with the basket of shells; now cmpty. He does not see you. He is hurrying towards the setting sun. And the wave is coming from behind and you want to run, but however much you try, you cannot, your legs are too heavy. You are lifted to the top of the hill but still there is no rest as you are carried upwards, higher and higher.

Eggshell

The road was icy but that was not unusual. Everything was packed under layer upon layer of hard ice; it had been for several months. The snow shoes for the tyres worked fine; their steel studs gripped the surface as May veered around the ruts. Her delicate cargo was next to her on the passenger seat and on the side of the box were printed the words 'For Vetinary use only'. The contents were silent, but then, they would be.

"Will you call in at the Farm shop on your way," he'd asked casually, "to pick up a few dead chicks?"

"It's for my end of year exhibition," her son continued. "We're doing an *afterlife* theme."

Well, that should be all right she'd thought, until now, when she was driving along with a box full of day old dead chicks. She didn't suppose the farm shop got many requests like that. After all, most people preferred their chickens to be alive and cute or if dead— plucked and ready for the oven without that in between stage—cute **and** dead.

The woman behind the counter had turned out to be Eva Hay; someone she had always sidestepped at the supermarket. She lifted her eyes to the ceiling when May explained what it was she wanted.

"There you are," she'd said handing her the box with a smirk.

"Enjoy!"

The box fell onto its side as the car rattled over a hump in the road. It was on the floor with the open end tilted down. Looking into the foot well she saw five, maybe six, dark fluffy bodies. Weren't chicks supposed to be yellow with red beaks like the ones you saw at Easter time? She shuddered when one of them moved, slipping down the back of another.

She had not seen the van approaching on the other side of the road, except that it wasn't on the other side because the road had turned into a single track lane on the approach to the bridge.

After the impact she stayed there, her nose pressed against the screen looking through a labyrinth of crystals. She was transfixed by the rhomboid weaving of the fine glass web but was unable to move because whenever she tried she felt a terrible pain shooting up her spine. It intensified with every second and her thoughts became like waving tentacles floating around trying to find a way out.

If only she had made that phone call straight after the argument and actually told Jo that she loved her. She had meant to. If only she had praised her for her success instead of saying nothing because of her own feelings of jealousy.

'If only, if only...'

None of it mattered now; not now that she was going to die.

The pain overwhelmed her, engulfed her in its blackness until it just as suddenly subsided and there was a light shining from above.

Perhaps that was it: she was dead.

The light was so bright that she had to lift her hand to shield her eyes from the glare. Or was she in heaven? She had never really believed in it, but it was certainly a relief to be out of the darkness. One minute she had been inside a dark tunnel of pain and now her body was free of all feeling and she was in the sunshine. Even the ice had melted away; in fact, there was no sign of it.

In front of her she could see a structure that she recognised. She had to think for a moment where she had seen it before. It was a key stone of a bridge with a carved emblem: she knew her history. It was one of the most important emblems of medieval heraldry – fleur-de-lys. She looked over the parapet and saw that below her flowed a wide river flowed. On its bank stood a willow; an elderly specimen with long yellow streamers that caressed the surface of the water. At the back of her mind came a nudge of memory. It must have been several years ago now that the ancient willow of Magden had been uprooted in the floods and swept away downstream. She remembered the headlines in the local paper, 'Centuries Old Tree finally succumbs to Climate Change.'

She blinked and stretched out her arms. With the exertion she wobbled and placed one hand on the wall; the wall of the old packhorse bridge.

None of it made any sense.

Despite all the efforts of the Society for Rural Perpetuity (aka SRP)—she had been the Secretary for three years—the bridge had been replaced a decade ago. It was part of the deal made between the Council and the building contractors when they were negotiating the plans for the new housing estate. The new bridge had been built in the modern style with steel girders and ugly concrete plinths much to the chagrin of the older residents. Now here she was on the very bridge that she and other members of the SRP had once stood, waving their banners, chanting and causing a blockade until they were arrested and charged with affray.

Through the soles of her boots she felt the nubs of the old cobbles. She had been wearing boots all year because the ground had remained so hard and frozen that to wear anything else would have resulted in a bone cracking slide. So many people had suffered broken bones that special fracture clinics had been opened. Right now, her feet were swollen and uncomfortable; the fur lining that had kept her feet snug during the winter months

63

made them sweat with the unexpected heat.

Everything was strangely quiet.

There was no traffic. But then it was the middle of the afternoon and not usually busy. She felt inside her pocket for her phone but remembered leaving it on the kitchen table in her hurry to leave the house. She took off her thick jumper and tied it around her waist and loosened the collar of her blouse.

She walked along the bridge expecting to turn right and cut through the estate of semi-detached houses towards the centre of Maggs. She was bound to see someone she knew. If not, she would go to the post office where Debs worked. She'd know what was going on.

The field on her right was full of meadow flowers: red poppies, blue cornflowers, purple loosestrife and creamy meadowsweet. May breathed in through her nose, enjoying the scented air. Beyond the field she could see the village church where a ferocious battle had been fought in the twelfth century. The result of the bombardment had left the tower in need of a prop. In recent years the prop had been replaced with scaffolding while surveys had been undertaken by the engineers. The tilted belfry had become a well known local feature and was depicted on badges and notebooks in the tourist office and even the road signs on entering and exiting the village had an illustration of a tilted tower.

Today, the tower was perpendicular.

May felt a sense of disorientation but as she walked towards the centre of the village she breathed a sigh of relief as she recognised the buildings but they were not quite how she remembered.

She was glad that the local town council had made an effort to keep the original features of the village and not to allow the use of modern building materials, the rendering of historical buildings, concrete, constructions over a certain height, or gaudy signage or flashy lighting as is common on the High Streets of the modern town centres.

For some reason, everything seemed smaller than she remembered. It was as though the huddle of buildings were now concentrated in a small area and were concealed by a tumble of stalls. There were traders of all kinds: cobblers, patternmakers, basket makers and spinners, cart wrights and fletchers, candle makers and musicians. As she turned one corner she passed a scribe at his work, quill in hand while a toothless citizen stood over him watching the magic appear. It was all just how she would have imagined a re-enactment scene of a medieval market place. It would make a perfect film set.

She knew there had been plans in the pipeline for a Medieval Day but as an expert of Local History she would have expected to be consulted. They had obviously gone ahead with their plans regardless, either that or a film crew had taken over the village again. It wouldn't be the first time. In any case, she had to admit, that they had done a very good job. Certainly, the smells were appropriate. Rotting vegetation and animal excrement in this heat made her feel quite nauseous. She pulled her scarf over her mouth and nose.

Behind the first market stall, a woman was standing with her hands on her hips, arms akimbo. She was wearing a mob cap and an apron made of coarse woven fabric which was tied around her waist. She realised that it was Eva Hay. Why her again, she thought? In front of Eva were several baskets of eggs and a ragged collection of hens in rustic basketry cages. She seemed to be absorbed in conversation with a woman who had a shawl closely drawn around her head and shoulders. Every now and again Eva would lift one hand and point in the direction of the bridge.

May listened but could not catch her words; only that their meaning was of a serious nature as Eva smashed her right fist into her left hand as if demonstrating an action of some violence. The two women were speaking with an accent that she was unfamiliar to May which surprised her as she had lived in the area for most of her life and prided herself on being able to tell the subtle differences between one village and another; by the lifting of a vowel or the leaving out of an end consonant. Perhaps she was losing her hearing. It had happened to her mother, along with the general confusion, but not until she was quite elderly. May coughed to try and draw their attention. Eva turned towards her but then seemed to be looking right through her just as May was wondering if their recent bonhomie would continue.

"Very authentic," she said out loud.

She was surprised at the volume of her own voice. Nevertheless, Eva took no notice; she actually seemed to ignore her. She simply turned back to her customer and carried on talking and began to place egg after egg into the proffered sack.

"Whoever invented egg boxes had a good idea, eh?" May tried again.

Still there was no response.

The woman had always been quite rude and May came to the conclusion that she was one of those people that blew 'hot and cold'. She wouldn't let it affect her—it was no great loss after all.

She studied the hens in their cages and the trays of straw that contained the eggs, eggs that would have no chance of hatching. She thought of the box of dead chicks and the one that was still alive and how its head had lifted upwards, its beak half open as if begging for a chance of survival. She thought of Jo, her family, her son, and how much she would miss them all, and even her neighbours. She had to get back before they missed her too. She knew that the only way was to go back the way she had come; then she could not get lost. For some reason she could not fathom, it was imperative that she should save the little bird.

Back on the bridge, Officer Blaine took a moment to assess the situation. Everything was icing over before they could move it. A generator had been brought in to apply heat to the freezing conditions but the melting ice soon froze over again making the bridge an even more dangerous place. He was concerned for his crew and was just about to call it a day. The crew was in the process of sawing through the final section of the car.

It fell apart with a crack.

The process had taken longer than it should have but with the woman trapped inside they had to go carefully. She might not be alive—they knew that—but it was still worth a try. The sides of the car were prised open and the ambulance crew were waiting with a stretcher. When the woman was finally lifted out there seemed to be little sign of life but the paramedic thought he could detect a faint pulse. Within minutes the patient was wrapped in heat pad blankets and slipped into the ambulance. The crew departed leaving Blaine to inform the authorities and check that the bridge was safe to open to the public again.

A weak sun was reflected on the icy tiles of the new houses and for a few moments Blaine stood alone. As he looked across the scene of the accident his eye caught on the carcass of the vehicle. He went over to it. Already there was a cover of hard ice over the open shell, as if a can of varnish had been poured over it. He was about to walk away when something caught his eye. He put his hand in and lifted it out. He smiled at the creature in his open palm. As he gently rubbed his thumb against the chick's heart, it gave a pulsing tweet.

Poetic Licence

Like most things in life there are always exceptions. On this route it's No 1 Lawless Avenue with its garden akin to a scrap yard and an indolent pit-bull that waits placidly on the door step. The moment it sees me coming around the corner it stretches in a lazy but arrogant way, showing off its muscular frame and indicating its gender to the world. Slobber drools from a too fat tongue, one eye is tattooed open; alert to any form of life, be it meat or veg. He (and I assure you it is male) has that air of menace as is the way of all thugs. You know; the one that says I will kill you for no reason.

I take out my pen.

His bull neck twisting
Every ligament strains
Eyes red with mist.

I might be a poet but that doesn't mean I'm going to put up with being bullied. Today, instead of lobbing the post from the pavement I feel an uncharacteristic recklessness. I open the gate. He is caught off guard judging by the way his left paw slowly retracts, scratching the concrete step. His head rotates in slow motion, like an evil exorcist. I freeze. This is how a rabbit must feel when it is caught in the headlights. The flight impulse takes over. The gate clangs shut with the weight of his pelting body. I jam the rusty ironwork between myself and the beast but still I fear for my life as the points of his teeth catch my cuff. I feed him a few letters and a packet for good measure.

There have been complaints apparently; things have gone astray. It could be the inter-mail system and the boss is very apologetic. Of course they can't prove anything.

"It happens all the time," he says vaguely. "It's the sponsors – they have these day-to-day checks. They reckon can tell by the response if their advertising isn't reaching the target audience."

He's a good man, my boss; not cut out for management really. I've only been doing this job for a week and a half and he's prepared to give me the benefit of the doubt.

I walk along the main road where the old houses are set back behind laurel hedges. My heart rate has returned to normal. I'm not one for costume dramas but I can appreciate the romance of these places with their stucco facades, sweeping driveways and ivy covered gazebos. Of course, back then, my place would have been 'downstairs' hard at work from dawn to dusk.

The old gentlemen would turn in their graves if they could see their fine houses now; all chopped up into flats and bedsits. Some have been left to rot; their roofs raided for slate, lintels stolen, carved stone lions that have become goal posts in someone's back yard.

Here we have one of the grandest mansions; now a residential home for the elderly. I see that the wheelchairs are out today. All in a row along the dappled terrace; sun hats perched on nodding heads.

> *Crumbling autumn bones*
> *sap of life diminishing*
> *stones without mortar.*

An old gent greets me.

"Fine day for it," he says, "and what message do you bring from afar?"

He stretches out a gracious but withered hand. I pass

him a likely envelope— one with a silky red cover and a waxy seal. The others reach out their hands too and gratefully receive my gifts. One lady is crippled with arthritis so I pick out something that looks like it will contain the prospect of a win, a rush of gold that could sweep her away into the sunset on a cushioned deck at full sail. Her gnarled fingers trace the embossed lettering.

This company I work for is a big operation; almost like the old Queen's firm. On the other hand it is nothing like it. Since the 2020 triple coalition government, we have no rights, no appeal system, no pensions, nothing. It's like you're a machine. I laughed this morning when the boss went on about a 'pedometer'.

"Time and motion study," he says. "It's an old idea that they're bringing back."

He told me that it was his job to monitor the routes, fill in forms and send off a daily report.

"It's not like a real job anymore." He sounded apologetic.

Apparently, I'm to be the 'pilot study'. The lads started calling me 'Tracker' straight away.

I carry on along Bank Bottom and up the steep hill where the terraces fit the ridge of the land. Nowadays, they're all professionals who live around here; enjoying the historical connections without the discomforts. One thing's for sure: they won't be waking up to frost on the inside of the window pane, or putting their feet onto cold linoleum first thing in the morning. Now it's all integrated bathrooms, solar generated under floor heating and heat exchange systems where energy is re-circulated within the household. I lean against a wall and get out my pen and pad.

The Aga Royals
living remotely controlled
under a stripped beam.

Still, there's something quite satisfying about the sound of the drop and slide of an envelope onto polished Victorian tiles.

The Manager asked me for the name of my last boss. Apparently the references didn't match up. I told him that he'd retired now, gone to live abroad. Actually I only ever knew him as Fred Forty. That was his nickname—don't know why. I think he'd lost heart when everything went electronic. He took the opportunity of having a go himself. We were told that we could all be entrepreneurs. All his savings went on buying up the old equipment and trying to work the end of town that no one else wanted — the hard mail area.

There's a woman sitting on a wall. She's crying. Two men are lifting a white leather sofa into the back of a van. Another one coming out of the house has an eyebrow missing. It's been replaced with a scar. He is laden down with a variety of gadgets, wires trailing. I guess she might have overstretched herself but you can hardly blame people, what with all the free credit you get offered these days.

Sign on the line, no fee
Credit where credit is free
In debt forever you'll be.

I know what's in a lot of these letters. If I knock on a door and it's followed by a twitch of a curtain and then complete silence, I know it's a debtor's demand. I write 'return to sender' on it and pop it back in the bag. I keep them safe. I've quite a few at home. I mean, why should people suffer? It's on the news all the time: unemployment black spot, more benefit claimants, highest levels of child poverty. We've all got to do our bit haven't we?

After a year Fred told me that it wasn't a fair market anymore; he couldn't compete. People just complained all the time until finally they'd change their hard copy service provider. It wasn't his fault if there were gaps in the system. The thing is he was only trying to do people a favour, give them a bit of choice. Isn't that what they're supposed to want? The problem was the big boys. They had it all sown up. He told me all about it; took me into his confidence. That was just before the auditors came in. Turned the place upside down they did. Poor Fred!

I like post cards. They're a rare treat these days. Some might call it nosy but you've got to have some perks. I think about all those journeys people take, proper journeys, abroad, to foreign places, so I take a lot of notes. That way, I'll know all the best places.

This attachment is rubbing my ankle something rotten but I'm nearly done now. One letter left in the bag. I see it's for Mr Chance back at Ample Drive. I passed by there a while ago and now it means going all the way back. It hardly seems worth the effort. Anyway, I can't because it'll make me late and my pay gets docked for every minute, and now probably for every unnecessary footstep picked up by this device.

It's one of those pre stick envelopes, the ones that don't stick at all. I've not heard of Llamazilla Travel before and it needs a signature. It looks like it might be an air ticket. I'll take it round there tomorrow, or whenever. I'll keep it safe for the time being. In any case, we've all got rights; rights to dream at least and sometimes in life you've got to take your chances. I wonder if air miles can be clocked on a 'pedometer'.

Seraph

The news on the radio had seemed unreal during those final days. The discussions were all about how the government was handling the strikes, whether it was right for the army to take over the fuel supplies, how much longer the food trucks would be able to get through. Then there were the reports of flooding and desertification in other countries, until finally all importation of food came to a halt. The food chain was broken and there was no hope of it being mended.

Emma had been watching out for the soldiers from an upstairs window. They came in trucks and tanks; their hoods pulled over their heads, they were shrouded in white bodysuits, their faces snorkelled in breathing masks. The choking stench of burning oil pervaded the air. As they trolled through the fields, they crushed everything, setting the land on fire, purposefully destroying the rancid crops. The yearlong rains had turned the fields into lakes of silvery mildew.

When Emma arrived at the centre she found that some people had already been there for a year. The place had the look of a medieval settlement from some ancient chronicle. It was an old fort and had purposely been built in a gothic style. Around it, in a horseshoe shape were ramshackle shacks, a leaning fence made from torn down saplings, and the ground was ankle deep in a mixture of mud and straw. There were two goats, a pig, and a few chickens. The goats roamed freely within the bounds of the fort but the pig had its own pen. There were also bunk houses whose walls consisted of plastic sheets and left over hardboard, and shelters, like large benders threaded with branches and reeds. The latter were only useable when the dry season eventually came.

The plateau of land that now contained their home had

been an Iron Age Fort and Burial Ground many centuries before and it was situated on a narrow strip of land, high up between two ranges of hills and had the advantage of being an all round vantage point; the perfect place to observe an approaching enemy. Because of this unique geographical position and by a quirk in nature it had been saved from the freakish weather systems that had been assaulting the rest of the country, and indeed, the northern hemisphere. By existing within a microclimate the refugees found that they were able to grow a few crops, albeit with a low yield, and mainly root vegetables. A source of clean water came from a borehole that tapped into a deep underground stream. This had originally been used to service the water feature in the courtyard by the entrance but the original stones from the fountain had long since been dismantled and used to shore up the walls of the main building. Now, it had become the means to a vital water supply for scores of people, a proper well had been built around it and buckets that could be lowered. These could be lowered simultaneously and winched back to the surface, dripping with sparkling fresh water.

The main building had a ladder that stood on the outside of the walls and went up to a turret. It was formerly a lookout tower and when it was Emma's 'watch' she could survey the land and watch the thin line of newcomers making their way to the shelter of the fort. They came with tales of survival: how they'd crossed the prairies, camped out in the deserts with the dingoes baying for their blood, negotiated the frozen tundra; navigated by the stars, the rising and falling of the moon, the ebb and flow of the tides, even by the shifts of flocking of the birds. These people were survivors.

The fort had once been a folly, a rich man's fantasy, and not built to be properly inhabited. The walls were made of a single skin of stone stuck together with loose mortar and many of them had fallen down with the severe frosts. Fragments of rendered stone lay dismembered, scattered along the steep sides of the hill. At its centre was the domed roof that had survived the pummelling storms of space debris that had pierced the atmosphere. When the sun was shining, the dome could be seen from miles around, twinkling with the tiny chips of malachite and sapphire that were embedded in its mesh covering.

The interior of the dome was like a Roman Basilica; fine plasterwork etched with winged angels and subtly painted in pastel shades. Emma had seen such cherubic creatures once before on a visit to the Sistine Chapel. The brochure had described them as being of the highest order of angels; the seraphim. On seeing these, Emma was filled with a sense of peace as she gazed at the placid faces as she recalled happier, easier times. Her child had been born when the world was tipping over on its side and although she knew that it would never be the same again she sometimes believed that if she closed her eyes for long enough, that when she opened them, everything would all go back to how it was.

It was with this sense of denial that she had avoided the Office of Registration. Her baby had never been official, never given a number, never been registered for the services that had eventually become nonexistent. Somehow, Emma thought that she would be safer by remaining anonymous. She simply called her, 'Babe', or 'Sweet Pea,' but now, inspired by the paintings of the dome, she decided it was time to give her child a proper name and that name would be Sera, in honour of the seraphim with the painted wings.

Sera was an easy baby. She never complained about anything but then she hardly had reason to. Emma kept her by her side, day and night, and if she as much as mewled, Emma would comfort her, feed her, play with her; give her what it was she required. Sera suckled from Emma's breast more and more, quite voraciously at times, clinging to her nipple with her gummy jaw between gasps of air. She thrived and it showed in her bonny face; a healthy glow, long dark lashes, a rosebud mouth framed by luscious pink cheeks. She put on so much weight that her ankles and wrists were bound in several rolls of flesh, her buttocks dimpled. Her feet were oyster soft pads that she kicked up in the air, chuckling and gurgling with delight.

Every evening, Emma snuggled down with her baby in their large sleeping bag; one she had sewn from two thick fleece blankets. She could tuck the edges in, keeping all the warmth inside and together they would be cosy and safe from the world outside. As Sera suckled, Emma wrapped herself around her baby, rubbing her nose into the nape of the neck, kissing and nuzzling her little chick. It was like being inside a warm silk nest.

In the daytime Sera got around by shuffling her bottom from side to side. She became so adept that once or twice there were cries of alarm from Emma when she found that she was not where she had left her. Somebody always found her having got stuck beneath a bed or outside in the yard scooping handfuls of dirt into her mouth. Once, she got inside the chicken coop and was found surrounded by chickens. They were all around, clucking and pecking the ground and she was right in the middle of them, lifting her arms up and down by the elbows, calling and smacking her lips together as if trying to emulate their calls.

The chickens had been there before the influx of this latest population and had only survived the axe because of the foresight of someone who'd thought it might be a good idea to save enough of them for future breeding. That first year there had been wolves from the mountains in the East who had come for an easy kill. They stood three feet high at the shoulder and when they came at night, their grey razorbacks caught in the moonlight like sharpened blades, their mouths dripping with hunger.

One morning Emma woke to find that she was alone inside her blankets. She called out, "Sera, Sera."

The other beds in the cabin contained only the sleeping forms of the other inhabitants. The door to the outside banged. It must have blown open in the night and with the light of the full moon the child had been drawn to it like a moth and made her way outside. Then, perhaps, the door had shut again leaving her outside.

Emma was outside, calling and calling. Others joined her, rubbing their bleary eyes, searching under the cabins, behind the disused vehicles, even around the well; peering into its dark eye.

No sign.

The only difference in the camp was the silence. No calling cockerel, no chickens bickering. Nothing. They must have been raided in the night and every fowl had been lifted clean away. There was no sign of a struggle; not a single chicken feather or a drop of blood marked the ground. But there was something, snagged on the perimeter fence: a single feather, buzzing in the wind.

It was the plume from a killer eagle's tail.

That day, the rains began. They fell to Emma's tears. Several days passed and the child was not found. The searchers had come up with nothing. Emma had to do something and there was still one vehicle that had been kept serviced.

Now Emma's hands were clenched around the steering wheel. If she loosened her grip they would stay there, stuck with sweat and fear. She had been driving all day. The young volunteer at her side was tapping a rhythm on the dashboard. His iPod was wired into the cigarette lighter and all she could hear was the buzz that circled the hive of his head. The plugs in his ears kept him within the safety of his own head, shutting her out, but she did not mind. She had only one thing on her mind and that was to find Sera.

Ahead of them were the Greystone Hills, their ridges lay like broken backbones across the horizon, shuttered by the clouds that drifted across the moon leaving silver trails of light. They stopped at intervals to scour the land, seeking every clue; prints in the soil, watching for movements in the gorse, sniffing the air for hints of carrion. Now, they were at the nesting grounds, where she believed they would find the killer eagle.

At least the rain had ceased.

The car swerved as Emma stabbed at the brake. They both peered through the slits in the muddy windscreen and she pointed to a gap in the trees.

"Let's camp over there?" she said. "We could head up into the hills in the morning when it's light."

Without waiting for a reply she pushed the gear stick into first, revved the engine and off they set, hopping and jolting over the ruts in the track. There was a derelict farmhouse further along and to the right of the building was a circle of white stone, a hooked rope dangled from a wooden arm.

"A well," she announced. "It could still be polluted, though," she warned.

The well was obviously disused and covered in a pile of sticks, twigs, fronds of grass. Bracken sprouted from its sides. The farmhouse was a skeleton; its bones were the rafters, its belly full of dark shapes but even so, it looked empty.

"It's too risky to light a fire," she said. "We'd better sleep in the back of the truck."

Emma stood by the driver's door for a moment, watching the shapes in the dark, assessing the movements of the trees until she was distracted by the sound of a trickle of pee hitting the back wheel. Once they'd unloaded the truck, she lifted the hatch door on the floor of the vehicle. They had one rifle between them, a .33, and a single string of bullets. It was the only one that had been found at the fort. On their way they had stopped at a derelict fuel station and siphoned some petrol from the stacked up cars. The lad had climbed through the fence and returned with a rusty blue bottle. He had smiled as she shook the liquid gas.

Only the bleak silhouette of the gutted farmhouse stood between them and the stars as the tiny blue flame flickered at their feet, yellow sparks snapping at the air. Crouching around the flame, she cut up the salted meat and threw it into the pan with a few of the earth onions they'd taken from the mountain. As she added a few drops from her water bottle and the leaves of wild garlic, the aroma drew saliva into her mouth. After they'd eaten, the lad lay sprawled on a blanket, gazing up at the stars, his foot tapping to a tune in his head. Emma picked up the gun and climbed onto the roof of the jeep and sat cross legged, perched on the roof bars, the gun over her lap.

Silence. The grey lights of the moon illuminated the farm and from here she could make out the original shape of the fields, now filled shoulder high with bracken and gorse. As the wind got up, the clouds skittered across the surface of the moon, clearing and darkening at intervals.

It must have been an hour or so later that it happened, just when her eyelids were slipping and her vision faltering; she struggled to stay awake. Emma had not slept since Sera had disappeared. She merely fell into a series of black holes. In her desperation to stay awake and on the alert, she would become caught in a net that bound her in its mesh and the more she twisted and turned the more she would become snagged and imprisoned. Rising in panic she would surface and shout until she was free of the darkness. Then with the realisation of where she was and what had happened, she would lay there sweating and cold. All she felt was pain in her heart.

Now, her collar had begun to creep up her neck, her breathing had slowed and her breast nudged against the butt of the rifle. She was slipping into the gap between sleep and wake, falling, falling, and before she reached the bottom she was jolted back by a sound; a shuffling scraping sound over by the farmhouse.

Something was moving out there but she could not make it out, she could not be sure of what she was seeing. She listened hard, breathing in shallow gulps, but all she could hear was the purr of breath coming from Will's open mouth.

There was the outline of the farm buildings and the tree nearby. And silence. Even the wind had dropped. The skin on her neck tightened. Her ears and eyes unfastened. She gripped the rifle. It was fully loaded.

Something moved in the dark. It was by the well. She wondered if it was an animal, a lone bear, oblivious to danger. Could it be a wolfhound? It was not tall enough to be a man. But there it was again.

Now she was a wire stretched taut, every vibration played along its surface. Her finger was on the catch as she held the barrel close to her body to bury the sound of the bullet entering the chamber. She released it, slowly, while every filament of her being was on alert. One more movement and she would send the bullet out there into the unknown.

Now, she had the dark hump in the sight, her single eye line. It moved. She raised her rifle to bull's eye.

Just at that moment the moon flashed through the clouds and revealed her quarry. She saw the eagle sitting on the pile of twigs on top of the well and she fixed it in her sight. The bird was dropping pieces of food, raw meat, into the nest. She would shoot the eagle and its baby. As she watched, wanting to get a perfect bull's eye, the baby bird raised its head and then its body. The body was plump, featherless, and it had a face. Not the face of a bird but the face of a child, a young child, hardly more than a baby, but more than anything it was a face she recognised. As it turned, it looked straight at Emma, but did not smile. It was a face of fear, pupils dilated, fixed, immobilised. Emma followed the gaze to the hand that had the finger on the trigger; her finger.

With sudden movement, a fluttering, the image in front of her blurred. It was then that she saw the wings, whisking upwards and lifting the child until it was level with her eyes and then the wings folded slowly down onto the back of the child, setting it gently back into the nest of the well.

Emma collapsed, slipping from the bars, letting the rifle clatter onto the metal roof.

"You OK?" It was lad's voice. "Do you want me to take a turn?"

But Emma could not speak. As she began to breathe, she relived that moment; that brief second in time.

As she held her hand up in front of her face, her trigger finger started to move. She commanded it to stop but she no longer had control. She could hear the pull, the click and the torpedo launch of the bullet leaving the rifle. She saw the spark from the shot moving through the air and entering the child's flesh. Sera's flesh. Then the writhing slump. And in her hands: a smoking gun.

She looked over to the place where the moon had pierced the curtain of cloud. She expected to see the child, her child, a seraph, frozen in fright. But there was nothing, just the silhouette of a broken well.

Where the Blue Line Fades

Mother will be at home and although it is still early in the day she will have capitulated. On the kitchen table will be an open bottle next to a half empty tumbler. Her eyes will be glassy with laughter or tears, but either way, I am glad I am not at home to hear the tale.

She blames me.

Today was meant to be the happiest of my life. Now, there is nothing left.

In front of me the peat smoke curls up from the chimneys making the world shimmer as if it is about to disappear by magic.

If only.

I breathe in the salty breeze; even the air is scented with memories.

Out across the bay a prison ship is leaving the safety of the stone harbour. As I watch it tilling the waves I wonder if Father is aboard. Will he look back? The boat catches the wind and with each rising it flickers in the sunlight until it has passed through the breakwater and out into the deep water channel. I screw up my eyes until it is gone, lost in a sea of flashing mirrors.

Mary is running up to me. She is crying again. Large tears roll down her face running one into the other.

"Will you stop it, stop crying'," I say.

I look down at her shin, crimson with blood, yellow with curls of scraped skin.

"Here, use this," I say and pass her my handkerchief.

The other children are running around in circles. They are chasing the blue butterflies who feed from the flowering gorse. They flitter just out of reach. Little Joe Finn smacks his hands together then stops in mid stride to slowly open them. His faith is shattered; his hands empty. Then he leaps up to chase the absconding butterfly. How I wish I was that butterfly; to feel the joy of escape and free flight.

I tuck my cold feet up under my skirt where they can warm against my thighs. A corner of the ticket digs into my side. I allow it to pinch my skin.

I will not forget.

In any case, I see it as clear as if it were happening now.

Don is standing in the shadow of the doorway doing a jig. He has a triumphant look on his face as he waves the tickets in the air.

"Let me see," I say but he holds them up just out of reach. He catches me and pulls me into his arms. He is kissing me over and over, one arm stretched up high.

A figure is coming up the steep path now and I think for a moment that he has come back but it is Johnny striding in that familiar way. Finally, he is over the ridge and entirely silhouetted against the sea as if fearlessly walking a tightrope.

I pull my skirt further over my legs. I see the frayed edge from the corner of my eye where a ribbon has fallen free. My hair lies loose on my shoulder, wavering in the breeze.

"She's on her way," he says, pointing to where the ocean meets the sky. "Look over at the horizon."

The others have gathered around and we peer into the filtering light. Little Joe is the only one not interested. He has fallen with the straps of his breeches caught around his arms and he is pushing his finger under a rock to release a swarm of ants.

"She'll be here within the hour," Johnny says.

I can't see anything but if I screw up my eyes I make out a speck at the place where the blue line fades into the mist.

Mary is pulling at my hand.

"See boat, see boat," she says.

She understands so well for all her four years.

"Want a piggyback, do you Mary?" Johnny asks.

She whoops and holds up her hands.

"Come on then," he says, swinging her up onto his back.

She clings to his shoulders and giggles as he turns around and around.

The others are already running down towards the quayside. Before long we are squeezing our way through a mass of people. We stop at a stall where shellfish are laid out in scalloped shells. My sister takes a cockle then puts out her tongue and wrinkles her nose.

We follow in the wake of the push carts piled high with crates that judder precariously on the cobbled concourse. I hear the playing of an accordion and half expect to see Uncle on his stilts, playing the tipsy clown as he does at Carnival time.

Behind us, the gaping warehouses are lined with barrels and crates. Men linger with their caps pulled down, cigarettes hang from their mouths. The women from Montgomery Street are here too and the mothers usher their children in arcs around them. The smell of beer is everywhere, sweet and cloying in the air.

The bells of the great cathedral begin to clang.

Sirens and horns reverberate from all around.

A man in a top hat is giving instructions to a porter. I see country folk and at their feet are boxes and cases tied with string, bursting at the seams.

We are carried along with the crowd.

When I first see her out beyond the harbour, I am alarmed. If she keeps coming towards us we will all be crushed to death. She is as large as the islands in the bay and moving towards us, horns blasting right through the body of the crowd.

I look around me, to my left and to my right.

Mary is not there and neither is Johnny. I imagine

Mother's face when I try to explain that she is safe with him but Mother will only scream that he is the brother of Donald, as if I need reminding.

The crowd eases back taking me with it. The dock workers attach ropes to the harbour cleats and wind the remainder into snakes of coiled mats. The tenders are lined up along the pier ready to take the passengers out to where the great ship is anchored. Laddered gangways fold out like opening wings and the crowd moves me forward.

As I look down at the narrow gap between boat and harbour wall I see the black water. Each time the waves rock the vessel, the gap narrows. It is as if my head is being squeezed of all memory except one.

I hear that terrible sound, the guttural bellow. I feel the push and then the hard ground. I am gasping for breath and when I looked up I see Father; his fists clenched, the muscles around his jaw twitching.

"She'll never go with the likes of you." His voice is a choked whisper.

"She will too. We love each other and will soon be wed." That is Donald's voice; my strong brave Donald. He is standing up to Father with a pride that stretches every fibre of his body. I see the fear in his eyes and then I see the reason: the slant edge of a knife caught in the moonlight.

I shudder and find that I am standing at the edge of the harbour. If I fall I will be crushed between metal hull and stone wall. I imagine what it might be like to plunge down to the harbour floor and look up at the whale of a shadow. I could slip away and no one would know.

I would be free forever.

The Band strikes up a tune, a jolly tune, one that makes me want to dance, despite myself. There is a long queue at the entrance to the walkway. People are talking, laughing loudly, too loudly. Others are gathered on the quayside shielding their eyes as they peer out to where the great ship is anchored. Some are dancing to a fiddler's tune as if determined to make the occasion a happy one.

I feel a hand on my arm. Johnny is at my side.

"Mary's gone home with the others," he says. "She'll be fine."

We are quiet for a moment. He sighs.

"Donald should have been here," he says, looking straight at me. "Is that what you're thinking?"

I nod and squeeze my hand around the ticket. I think about the gap and the coiled ropes and the black waters that suck and suck.

Johnny's voice is quiet as he speaks.

"Donald gave me his ticket before he died."

I look into his eyes. They are welling like an ocean swells with waves. I feel nothing as he takes my arm and together we walk onto the pier. The skipper checks our tickets and hurries us along the gangway. We are the last passengers to board the tender. The strangers on the quay are waving but as I look towards the open sea, my eyes are dry.

Inside the Pony

"Oh aye, it'll be a rough crossing," the man said, "what with all the white horses out in the bay!"

Mother ignored him but Evie had noticed that he had been watching them ever since they had boarded the boat. It was getting dark now. Mother was staring out of the window but it was as though she was seeing nothing, not even her own face. Evie drifted into sleep and dreamed she was floating on a raft and when she looked over the side she could see a face staring back at her from beneath the surface of the water. She reached out but as her fingers broke the surface it disappeared and her hand merely scooped up a stream of seaweed.

Her blanket slipped from her knees and woke her. The lights had been turned low and everyone else was slumped on their seats, dozing, snoring or restlessly shifting from one side to the other. Evie tucked her pony into her jacket. She thought about the conversation she had overheard the night before. Her Mother had been talking to Aunty Kath on the phone; her tone was low, her words gravelly like she had sand in her throat.

"He can take a running jump if he expects me to hang around," she'd heard her say. "No, no, Cath. He should have thought about that first. It's not fair on Evie."

At the sound of her name she had held her breath, listening more intently, while her pony grazed on the carpet. The gymkhana was set up with its hurdles of saved up lollipop sticks and an ashtray filled with water for the pond.

"He's refusing to tell them. He won't say a thing."

After a while Evie picked up the pony and began to comb its hair. As the brush flew over the nylon mane, the deft strokes caused flicks of static to prickle in the dusty hallway. Her mother looked up and she closed the door.

Earlier, they had caught the bus to the other side of town. It was Evie's first visit to the castle. From the great plaque at the entrance the lion had gazed imperiously at her, the eyes piercing beneath the rim of a golden crown. She wondered why the unicorn had chains around its body while the lion stood free on its hind legs, its front paws stretched up and along the side of the Queen's crest.

Evie held tightly on to her mother's hand as they walked under the arch of the old fortress. The building had no windows on the ground floor, just blocks of brick that were lighter than the surrounding stone and the walls rose to a great height. She almost fell backwards before she could see the entire building with each of its jutting angles reaching for the sky. At the top of each buttress there was a turret and from it an open mouthed drain which was held up by a pair of great stone paws, claws with long nails.

Several people from the bus were filing towards the same entrance in ones and twos. She felt sorry for the boy who was crying. He was so upset that he did not seem to care about the rivulets of snot that were rolling over his top lip. His mother was dragging him by the hand but his body was twisted back as if all he wanted to do was to go in the opposite direction. Finally, she smacked him; the shock abruptly stopped his wailing just long enough to be yanked up the steps of the entrance.

All around them were guards. Their steel brimmed caps stood proud of their faces, they all had the same expressions, blank and inscrutable. They wore navy blue uniforms with brass buttons and Evie noticed that they were embossed with the same crest that she had seen at the entrance, the one that was repeated on every signpost. Around their waists hung chains with large metal loops that held a multitude of keys.

Last term, Evie's class had been learning about the

Normans; how they had invaded the town hundreds of years ago, climbing up the walls with their shields and spears and longbows and they heard how the townspeople had gathered in the courtyard at the centre of the fort and how the soldiers had repelled the invaders, showering them with arrows from the slit turrets.

At the end of each day, Mrs Pearce read from a story book. Evie's father was living at home then and Evie told him one of the stories. It was about a beggar who had disguised himself as a baker in order to pass through the castle gates. He had planned to steal the Queen's jewels and Evie carefully explained to her father that stealing was wrong. He laughed and told Evie that sometimes people had no choice especially when they lived in a country where everything was unfair and that some people who never worked were rich and others who worked very hard had nothing at all.

"Anyway," he'd said, his voice going quiet. "Everyone has to make a living somehow, and..." He muttered under his breath. "I've never hurt anyone, not even a fly."

The people from the bus were in the waiting room, perspiring together within the same four walls. The boy, now mute, stared at her with round unblinking eyes even when she poked out her tongue. Around her she could smell the sharp tones of perfume that cut through the greasy accumulation of sweat and smoke. The man opposite kept flicking his fingers and she noticed the dark yellow stains. It reminded her of her uncle Rob. He was dead now. He'd been coming out of a bank one day and had walked straight out in front of a car. All the money had fallen out of the bags. It was a windy day and everyone in the street had stopped what they were doing to stare at the shower of paper money that descended all around. It was reported in all the papers. Her dad had made a collage of the cuttings and kept them in a frame.

"Not a bad way to go," her father had said.

"You'll see y' Daddy soon," the woman was saying to the little boy, her tone was more sympathetic, perhaps in respect to her audience. She pulled out an orange sweet from her handbag, took off the cellophane wrapper and popped it into the boy's mouth. Evie could smell the tangy scent of oranges.

Occasionally they heard the clink of keys in doors and the clunk of metal locks but when the guard came in, he pointed at Evie's mother.

"Not you," he said.

There were more checks to be done. Evie's father was an important person. She knew that because she had seen the words 'by appointment only' on the envelope of the letter that had come through the door, the one with the crest of the lion and the unicorn.

"Arms up," the guard told her mother. They were standing in small room that had doors at either end. Evie watched as her mother was searched. When it came to her turn she was asked to hand over her pony and the guard checked the roots of its mane and the pads of its hoofs. The woman guard smiled.

She did not know that the head came off.

Everyone was always interested in her pony. When the policewoman had come to the house, Evie had remained silent while they were sitting at the kitchen table.

"What a lovely pony!" the policewoman exclaimed. "What's its name?"

Evie hid the pony under the table and did not answer. The woman told Evie about the horse that she used to have as a child and how she liked to ride in the country. Evie was about to ask her more about it when they heard noises coming from upstairs. Her mother's voice was raised and the bathroom cabinet with the squeaky hinges was being opened. There was a whoosh of air as the loft space was opened at the top of the stairs. Evie gripped the ridge under the table and it rocked, spilling her drink across the surface. She could hear the others in the cupboard under the stairs. They must be very near the brass ring pull that was set into the floor and hidden under a rug.

"Hello, hello!" It was a man's voice. "What have we here?"

She remained silent, hardly daring to breath. She thought about the lunch time meetings at the edge of the school field. On the last occasion, he had reached through the break in the fence and squeezed her hand.

"Look after this," he'd said. "Keep it somewhere safe for me. And remember, you'll always be my princess."

When he had gone, she opened the palm of her hand and saw the piece of paper with the numbers and letters scrawled across it. There were no proper words and it did not make any sense.

As they went through to the visiting room, Evie blinked. The walls were white and the floor was a pearly grey that shone in reflecting strips from the high windows. They were right inside the big tower now where the blue sky was crossed with rows of iron bars. She noticed the flinch on her father's face when he saw that she was looking around the room. The tables and chairs were set out in neat rows, symmetrical, set in groups of four. Her mother tried to pull a chair forward but it was screwed to the floor.

The only thing that moved of its own accord was a fly that flitted from person to person. Evie looked around and saw that now and again someone's hand would slam down onto their table.

Evie slipped on and off the edge of her seat while her parents spoke in words that were too heavy for their tongues. The chair was plastic and cold, the toys in the box were old, the cars had their wheels missing and the plastic building blocks had indents that could only be teeth marks.

She went over to the vending machine where she could see everything in the room reflected in its tinted glass. For once, she was allowed to choose whatever she wanted but she could not decide, so she pushed the coins into the machine, closed her eyes, and pressed a button. When she opened them she saw that her parents were staring straight ahead. They were even deaf to the sudden thud as the machine delivered the extra strong mints into the tray.

When he was being led away, her father looked over the guard's shoulder. It was as if he was trying to say something with his eyes. They were filling with water.

Now she felt a prickling in her own eyes and the sea was becoming a blur of dark grey, as if her tears were mixing with the brine of the sea. She could no longer see anything through the cabin window.

Her mother had woken up and was talking to the man opposite.

"We just need a break," she said.

"Life gets stressful sometimes and you've just got to get away."

"Well, the island is about as far as you can get from the mainland," he replied. "Sort of place no one would think of looking for you."

There was something about the man that Evie did not like. His face looked as if it had been moulded onto his face. The buttons of his blazer were embossed with a lion and a unicorn.

As the boat slipped through the water Evie took out the

pony from under her blanket. She pushed her thumb into the ridge of its neck and slipped off its head. Yes, it was still there.

Map Woman

Matthew is sitting very still as if he has been struck. Caroline knows that he isn't really reading the newspaper; the one that he is holding up in front of him. In fact, he has not turned over the page for at least ten minutes. Over his shoulder she can see the words *Photography Competition* and *Next week's theme: Eyes of Nature*. Here is a way out of their silent stalemate. It is obvious to her that neither of them will give in. In any case, she's had enough of talking; they just go around in circles until there is nothing else to say. That's all they seem to do now.

She pushes her hands into the small of her back and yawns. To the dog, this movement holds the promise of a walk and he jumps up, eyes bright, tail wagging.

"The storm seems to have passed over now," she says. "I think I'll go out for a bit and take the camera."

"Mind if I join you?" Matthew asks.

The question lingers in the air.

She can hardly say no. After all, she has agreed that they should be civil to one another. It was never going to be easy.

Thirty minutes later they pull into the car park at Cape Mort. Here, the headland ends in an arch through which the sea explodes, bellowing like a prehistoric beast. This is where the Jurassic meets the Mesolithic, showing off its layers of sediment and displaying them like a text book illustration of planet Earth's history. It is deserted today just as it was before the advent of man and woman.

Thirty metres inland from the edge is a sign, its red lettering is weathered but still legible. 'Danger of Subsidence,' it reads and behind it there is a row of heavy wooden posts strung with barbed wire forming a fence that stretches across the headland, deterring all access. All that can be seen beyond the brier is a jagged outcrop of rocks.

Matthew and Caroline walk at a good pace, both enveloped in hooded waterproofs. He has the dog leash looped around his wrist. She carries a small rucksack and the camera, plus her recent investment; an expensive telephoto lens. Pan runs ahead, no doubt to follow the scented tracks of small creatures.

Another walker and a dog come towards them and they politely stand to one side.

"Good afternoon," Matthew says.

"Yes, it is, for now. More storms are due later on," the woman replies, "but first watch out for the mist coming in from the east."

She points out to sea but before they can look the dogs have taken their attention. Pan is rolling deferentially and the other dog is leaping and barking.

"He won't hurt," the woman says, "just likes to play."

There is an awkward moment when no one says anything.

"I wonder if you know where I might find these Standing Stones?" the woman asks.

She has opened out her map and is pointing to a place on it. "It shows them on here, quite nearby."

"I'm fairly sure there's not been another path going off, not for the last mile at least," Matthew says.

He turns to Caroline for confirmation.

"No, I've not seen one," she says.

She is almost reluctant to agree with him.

"You have an old map here," Caroline says. "The path might have disappeared. There's been so much coastal erosion that the path on the map might have completely subsided away."

Folding up the map and wishing them a good day the woman whistles to her dog.

Pan runs after her too.

"Hey, Pan, come back here," Matthew yells, but Pan does not even glance back.

Caroline has set off.

At the end of the day it's his dog. They walk on but after a few yards Matthew won't go any further.

"We'll have to go back," he says.

When they arrive at the headland a thick mist is rising from the sea. They watch as it swirls over the edge of the cliff and around the stones.

"Do you think these are the standing stones?" Matthew asks.

"Maybe," Caroline replies. "They do look very odd in this light."

Matthew coops his hands around his mouth.

"Pan, Pan..." he calls.

They hear a single bark but it is difficult to tell the direction from which it is coming. Caroline looks towards the headland; holds the camera against her chest and climbs between the wires of the fence.

"Hey," Matthew says, "I don't think that's a good idea".

"Please yourself," she says but she is already through to the other side.

He follows. When they reach the stones, there is so much bramble and gorse underfoot that the edge is unclear. Then she sees it; a chasm in the centre of the boulders; a sudden drop that goes through the middle of the cliff. Below them the sea is sucking in and out.

"Wow!" exclaims Caroline, "this must be how an arch is made."

Matthew's face is pale.

"Look how the cliff has dropped away while the sea

101

continues to erode the soft rock…" Caroline says.

She points to the sea beyond the cliff but he is not listening.

"..and then you're left with a strong pillar out on a limb."

She whistles. "It's so fascinating! It's like a huge eye looking up at us."

Her eyes are sparkling as she clicks her fingers.

"Eye! 'Eyes of Nature'; the theme of the Photography Competition."

"We need to find Pan before we do anything else," Matthew says.

"I'm going to take a few shots," she says, ignoring him, "just to see how they turn out."

Matthew calls for Pan again. There is no sound, no returning bark this time.

Meanwhile, despite the ground being so precarious underfoot, she has taken the camera out of its case and loaded a new film. Then she takes the tripod from the rucksack and stretches out its telescopic legs and jams the feet between the crevasses in the rock.

"That should do it," she mutters.

She screws the lens onto the front of the camera, braces her legs firmly against a rock and tilts the lens at a downward angle. Now the entire orbit of the hole is encompassed in the viewfinder. Little flicks of light play across the water below them as she adjusts the light meter.

"It could really do with a focus in the foreground to give an idea of scale."

She is excited as she looks through the lens.

"Crouch beside it Matthew and point your hand down at the sea and then look back at the camera," she says.

Reluctantly, he follows her instructions but quickly

stands up again as he almost loses his balance.

"How about if I jump over the edge and you use a slow shutter speed for that moment, you know, the one when I plunge to my death," he sneers.

"Very funny, Matthew," she says, "but maybe that's not such a bad idea."

"Huh, don't think I'm going to make it that easy for you," he counters.

She huffs.

"Can't you see I've got a really good opportunity here? Just hold onto that rock, then you won't fall."

If she has judged the light correctly she will have the perfect picture: a man at the edge of the world, a man gazing into the eye of a giant. And it really does look like an eye with the sea forming a ring of white foam as it slaps against the sides of the hollow, the deep green iris.

She takes several shots. Then she hears a bark from behind and looks around expecting Pan to nuzzle her arm. There is no dog, so she puts her eye back to the view finder and snaps the shutter. This time it is different. She looks at the empty scene.

"Matthew," she calls, "Matthew?"

As she lets go of the camera, it rocks on its tripod. She looks behind and all around her.

"Matthew. Matthew. Don't be silly."

There is no answer.

Slowly, she moves towards the edge of the abyss. A stone dislodges under her foot and ricochets over the cliff edge. There is no splash, no sound at all but the lapping waves in the chasm far below. The layers of mist are thicker now.

"Matthew," she calls; her voice is thin now, suppressed with fear.

Behind her the air is so thick that she cannot see further

than the length of her arm. No one else will be out, not if they've any sense, not in this fog.

She is on her own, really on her own.

"Matthew!" she calls again, assertively, as if this is his last chance.

She is answered by a single sound. She turns around and peers in all directions. Everything is so distorted that she cannot tell if it is a bark or a man calling for help. Then there is a darkening in the mist. It forms a human shape as it comes towards her.

"Oh, Matthew, there you are."

Already, despite her relief, she is sparking with anger but then she stops abruptly. It is not Matthew. Two dogs are running around the legs and one of them is Pan.

"You've taken some finding," the map woman says. "I thought I'd better bring your dog back. She wouldn't go back on her own."

She looks into Caroline's face.

"Is something wrong?" she asks.

Pan and the other dog are barking by the rim of the abyss.

"No," Caroline replies.

A few stones loosen from the edge and rumble down the side. This time there is a splash.

Wild Rose

The hotelier was apologetic but what could he do? What did they expect? It was their quiet period after all. In fact it was so quiet that they were lucky that they were even open. It was hardly worth keeping the hotel open let alone the restaurant especially in times like these when nobody had money to spend, not in a depression. When the hotelier had taken Kim's booking he had forgotten to mention any of this and now she was beginning to feel responsible but it wasn't her fault that the banks had crashed or that all the young people who would otherwise have been there working as waiters or waitresses on minimum wage had emigrated.

It was raining heavily when they arrived at the seaside town. A cold sea mist oozed from the north and the high tide meant that there was not even a slim corridor of pebbles left to walk along. Neither was it the vibrant place they had visited during their honeymoon all those years ago; no queues at the ice cream parlour, no children skipping in and out of the tide line or racing along the mile of white sand. The streets were their only option and many of the shops had closed down due to the recession, their signs left to rust and their paint to peel. In the only open cafe they warmed their hands around a cup of instant coffee (the type that was mixed with ground chicory and dandelion). All imports had been halted.

"I suppose we could go home," Paul suggested. "No harm done." He brightened. "We might even get a refund."

As they walked along the paved promenade, the rain seeped inside their collars.

"Oh, come on, we're here now." Kim's voice was brittle. "Can't we..." she faltered, "make the most of it?"

The glitch in her voice had only surfaced during the last

few days. Selling the idea to Paul that they should take a break away from home for a night had taken its toll. Organising everything at home, working out the budget, making the phone calls and all the chivvying along was an exercise in management that would have tested a professional. Paul on the other hand liked to keep a tight rein on the little money they had coming in. Depression or no depression, Kim knew they needed to escape, just for a short break. Their lives had become like the pond at the bottom of the garden, full of duckweed, stagnant. Their home no longer fitted the description on the sign over the gate and had not for several years. 'Chez Verve', was a misnomer if ever there was one.

Glad to retreat from the rain, they entered the hotel and hung up their raincoats on the empty coat stand. Kim went to the bar. At least this was well stocked. She ordered the drinks: two halves of snakebite—that had been the drink of the day when they were at college; and a couple of whisky chasers while she was at it—and a packet of crisps (for old times' sake).

"I think these might be out of date," Paul said, inspecting the first crisp he took out of the packet.

The woman behind the bar had turned her back to them and appeared to be transfixed by a huge television screen. The only programmes that played these days were the old soap operas and they seemed rather dated now. In this one a scene of domestic strife was unfolding. The woman actor had just thrown a diamond ring into the gutter.

"Do you know how much that cost?" the man asked.

"Is that all you care about?" The woman spat just as the ring tinkled through the grating.

The adverts came on. The usual ones: a pawnbroker's special offers, pattern cutting tools for making your own clothes etc. They were never promoting exotic holidays anymore or the

106

latest fashion in sofas or new style kitchens. Those days had gone.

Kim and Paul carried their drinks from the bar to the bench seat. It faced the window and they sat side by side, sipping their drinks, watching a stream of water spouting from a broken gutter in the diminishing light. The couple on the screen had returned and were now embracing and kissing with the intensity of an illicit affair.

Paul took out his mobile phone and looked solemn.

"No reception. Again!" He puffed. "I don't know what the point of having a mobile phone is anymore".

People were coming into the bar room now. A young woman with a shawl around her shoulders approached them. She was young and brightly dressed and she carried a basket over one arm.

"What lovely roses!" Kim exclaimed but Paul had already gone to the bar.

The basket was brimming with pastel pink wild roses, delicate, but their subtle scent filled the room. The girl reminded her of someone she had once known but she could not recall the name. The way she moved was familiar, assured and self-possessed, and the way the eyes sparkled gave the impression that her life was full of anticipation.

When Paul stumbled back he had a packet of peanuts sandwiched between elbow and body.

"Here we go," he said, slopping the drinks onto the table, "a romantic meal for two in an exotic location of your choice!"

His last words blurred into a single line as he slipped back into the seat.

"Our choice!" she reminded him.

Kim straightened the rose in her cleavage and mopped up the spillage with the beer mats. Sitting on the high stools at the bar were three people: two sullen looking men grumbling into their beer glasses, and a woman who was picking her ear with a little finger. She watched the woman study whatever it was she'd found there and then with a flicker of revulsion Kim took a swig of her drink and turned to look out of the window. Unfortunately, the line up at the bar was vividly reflected in the glass because the night had formed a dark backdrop. Paul was absorbed in reading the brewery facts that were printed on a sodden beer mat.

"This place needs livening up," she said.

"Anyone know a good song?" She was on her feet, addressing the whole pub—the three people at the bar and the barmaid.

"Kim," Paul hissed, "Sit down. You'll make a fool of yourself."

"Eh up," said the younger man; the one wearing the cap.

Paul tugged at Kim's arm.

Kim wavered for a moment but remained standing.

"Lisa," the cap man said to the barmaid, "how about turning that off and stickin' on the karaoke?"

He turned and shouted in the direction of Kim and Paul. "Let's have a party, shall we?"

The barmaid 'tutted' but turned towards the switches on the wall behind her and gave them a flick. As the screen went blank the karaoke machine rumbled into action.

The other man passed the microphone to Kim. As the music started she took out her glasses from her handbag in readiness for the words on the screen. Then it all stopped: abruptly. Just as Kim was about to open her mouth to sing, the bar was plunged into darkness as the power was cut. There was silence until they heard the strike of a match and a lit candle was placed onto the bar. Soon more candles were stuffed into empty bottles and a cosy blaze of light filled the room.

"Don't let it stop you," a voice came from the bar. "Go on love, you carry on."

Nobody minded that she had little sense of melody and at the end of each song they clapped enthusiastically. More people began to arrive. Better to huddle together than stay at home alone in the dark, someone explained. After some general exuberance and with the fortification of more drinks Kim felt encouraged to continue. Two songs later Paul suggested that she let someone else have a turn. That was when she lurched towards him, fell onto him and when he buckled she lost balance. They both toppled to the floor.

"I think I need another drink," she announced.

"Don't you think you've had enough?"

"As if you'd notice..." she slurred.

They had rolled over and tipped themselves up into a sitting position. Paul was about to remonstrate but he drifted off. Something had caught his eye. He was peering into Kim's cleavage.

"Where the hell did that come from?" he demanded.

Kim stared back at him, her mouth opened. Even in the semi dark she could see a flush blooming across his cheeks.

"I wish I'd brought my sunglasses," she said when they left the hotel the next morning.

She knew she had enjoyed herself the night before but to be honest she could not remember very much about it apart from the fact that there had been a party that had gone on late into the night. Inexplicably she had a creeping sense of dissatisfaction.

Perhaps she was simply exhausted. She knew that if Paul had had his way he would have spent the entire weekend in his shed. The respite care had been difficult enough to arrange. That was followed by the struggle she'd had trying to persuade her elderly and confused mother that she wasn't leaving her forever and that it was only for one night and that she would be well cared for. Then there was the guilt. Kim was good at guilt, always had been. Paul on the other hand was a realist; a man who stood by a rational decision to the bitter end whatever emotional turmoil might be unfolding around him or the fact that the world was changing inexorably. Glancing at him in the passenger seat, she saw that his face was placid, exactly as it had been when they'd set off from home the day before. His earphones were plugged in. No doubt he was listening to an audio book—most likely a biography about someone who'd had an interesting life.

Kim looked up at the rear view mirror. The face behind looked up and winked. It was a young face, exuberant, with a fresh complexion; the hair was fine, tousled, as if it had only ever run free with the wind. A brightly coloured scarf was slung around the neck, just the kind that Kim herself used to wear. In one ear was a single drop earring that swung with a rhythm that caught Kim's eye. She began to tap her index finger on the steering wheel as if to music, the music of her youth.

As she drove down the motorway she felt a sense of excitement as if the old pages of her life were closing. She checked once more in the mirror to see if the passenger was still there. She winked at her and opened the driver's window. The world around them might be changing but she wasn't going to be dulled by it or stay hidden away waiting for it to end. She watched as whole chapters of her life fluttered out of the window. Freed of their binding they littered the surface of the road.

Dancing with Sylphs

You are driving along a highway of evaporating tarmac, or so it seems by the way the heat haze obscures your view. The trees in the distance never get any closer; they wiggle around until they arrive at either side of the car. You know the night is about to draw in and that it happens all of a sudden in these parts, so you pull off the road and follow a track that goes off through the trees. You have already noticed the fuel gauge. Maybe it is faulty.

On your left is a steep gully where the balding tussocks look as if they have been bulldozed and dumped. Beyond them, the trees thin out and you can see a wide valley. It must have been an old river bed judging by the cracked surface, like the markings of a meandering snake. There is no sign of life – not even the rocky scatterings of the old sheep keeps from a hundred years ago. No sheep now — even they wouldn't survive.

Two birds are flying over you, slowly. They are looking down. They could be super sized egrets with their broad wingspan and large bills. They have seen you but they are heading out towards the horizon. Slowly they fly across the sun as if completing a scene from some old willow pattern plate. The egrets return. They have become luminous in the dead sunlight; their eyes dark hollows, cut outs in a silhouette.

Here is as good a place as any if you are going to sleep in the car. You get out and check the boot to see what is in there: a jack, a crowbar, an axe. You tear open the slice of chewing gum and stuff it into your mouth and enjoy the intense flavour of fake apple. Those other things might come in useful in any other circumstance; but without a blanket you will freeze when the dark closes in for the night. You get back into the passenger seat and hug your legs into your body and try to close your eyes. Then you switch on the radio. Nothing. Just the fuzz of boiled air eviscerating inside the radio. You turn it off and then you hear the click. You think it's just some kickback from the radio.

The shadows make shapes in front of you. Down the track they are moving, waving around, darting from side to side. Maybe they are bats but you don't think the bats have survived. The shapes become more defined and you are sure they are beckoning you to come out of your hidey hole, to follow them. Maybe there are people ahead, friendly welcoming folk. You are reminded of the parties in the old days before it all happened when a big group of you would go off into the mountains: set up the generator, stoke up the sound system, light the beacons and dance until your muscles seized up. Then you would have a feast.

It's no good. You are not going to sleep anyway. You open the car door. Slowly you make your way around to the boot which is on the catch, not locked. Now you have the crowbar in your hand and you are following the track, watching the moving sylph lights, slipping and hiding behind the trees. Their colours are tantalising—cadmium, ochre, rose, vermillion, slipping into magenta, sepia and indigo—and they are always in front of you.

Maybe there will be something to eat up ahead. You think about the cans, packets of dried food, stuff that might have been discarded. In the early days of the new life it was ok. It seemed there was enough tinned food to last forever; but then, even before it had run out, people were killing each other for a can of beans. But what are the chances of finding anything like that now? If there was any food around it would have been snatched up long ago. You might well think there is no one around in this outback. No one could survive.

You feel the blow to your back but you only understand what has happened when the breath leaves your body, when you are face down on the stony track, when a great weight is pressing you into the ground. The sound of tearing gristle is coming from

112

your face. Everything is bubbling, black, moist, almost pleasant. Your body has gone into shut down. It needs to work things out.

You have been hit from behind. You didn't see it coming and now the sting is filling your mind, your body is screaming out 'pain'. Your face pounds, the flesh around your eyes is swelling; you think your nose must be broken. The taste of metal fills your mouth.

Across your back is the trunk of a tree, a slim tree, not some old loose bark birch but one that still has life in its leaves. The light is almost gone and the colours that you were following have all disappeared. You lift yourself up with the effort of one who is on their last chance, arching your back until you tip the tree onto the road behind you and crawl to the edge of the track where the root of the tree is severed. It is then that you see the marks of the axe.

I could have told you not to come this way, down this track. I could have warned you, told you not to stop, don't leave the car. But I didn't.

I wanted to see what would happen because this is what happened to me, a long time ago. This is how I ended up being stuck in the Ugly Place. And now I have your axe and it will make my life a little easier. It's a hard life out here on your own. Some days I have actually begun to believe that there is no one else left on this earth, it's just me, alone. Me and them. All they do is tantalize, tease me. And then you come along like some old fashioned pudding; all sweet and innocent, and now, all mine.

I see you are wandering back up the track, zigzagging, acting a little concussed. That'll pass. So now you are heading towards the stream but you must know that you cannot drink the water. Everyone knows that, all who survived know that. If they did not know, they soon found out. I'm the lucky one who found the borehole made by the Indigenes. They knew a thing or two. They divined to find the narrowest layers of soft strata, pushed in their hollow straws to reach the clearest water from the streams that run between the layers of deep bedrock. It keeps me alive.

You're the first person to come along here in a long time. I don't know how long. It might be years for all I know. Maybe you'd heard about me or they sent you to look for me.

I thought it was a rifle at first, that thing in your hand. I tried to warn you. Don't say I didn't.

You have almost reached the stream now. You can hear the water, trickling down from the hills, the ash pile hills. Whatever you do, don't drink the water.

You are on the ground and you are not moving. You should never have come here. Don't say I didn't warn you.

The shadows have stopped. It must have been the moment the tree came down. The dancers have gone home, vanished like they do every night. I'll look after you, I promise. Tomorrow, we'll be dancing.

The Hanging Tree

I am their last port of call, the place where justice throws its pall over the face of the crime. I am the one who hears the final words of the perpetrator. I am the end point, my skill, the definition of precise action implemented, my act always complete. I am the master of my craft, perfected over time and time again in neat, discrete executions of duty.

But today I have taken my last guinea. I have cleared the decks, swabbed the bloodied boards. My life's work is complete and now I wish see the land I've so long cradled in my gallows' hand. I wish to breathe the air of peace in the country that now cries victory.

The dog is at my side as I walk the lanes. I have earned my freedom and I may go wherever I wish but first of all, I will seek the familiar paths through the countryside of my early life. The dog is restless, too close to my legs.

"Heel," I call.

Now he is barking at an animal in a field.

"Shut up!" I snap.

Then I see the cow with the loose skin and I reckon its weight is no more than that of a thin man. My thumb meets my fingers as I count the protruding vertebrae and listen to the hollow keys, a xylophone of ribs; that scrape along a defoliated hedge of thorns.

There are no birds. It seems that none have survived. There are no sweet caws or chirrups to lull me into falsity. Here is a cow with a painful sickness. The udders are too loose, mere veined bags that dangle in the sparse grass. The animal chomps in a regular unnatural graze, its eyes like blown glass are driven by a mad desire.

Something other has happened here while I have been at

my work; more than a spent victory or a battle of arms. The land is tinged, luminous, as if flushed under a high set sun, or sprayed with yellow crystals of a sulphurous kind. The crushed powder wafts from the cow's hoofs and with every step the grass crumbles into a bitter sherbet. The coarse dust catches in my throat and eyes. Even the dog sneezes and then nudges at my legs, pushing in front of me as if to prevent us from going any further. We turn and in silence go back the way we came.

It is with relief that we reach the highway and to recognise the places that we passed before we'd came to the broken place: the clump of yarrow, the splintered sign, the house in the dead trees with the blackened rafters, the hollow eyed windows, the chimney breast that lays naked, exposed to the blistering sun.

Now we are back at the crossroads of the hanging tree. The dog pees at the base of the gallows. The empty noose beats a rhythm, a drum roll. The dog is whimpering, keeping close to my heel, fearful, obedient to the end.

He barks when the rush of air ruffles his fur. A whirl of dirt spirals upwards as the platform drops and the sound of his howl echoes. I rise and slump. My feet swing to the creak. His eyes, his nose, are the last I see.

Runner

His hand felt for the key in his pocket. He was reassured by the weight of its ornamental ironwork. Nevertheless, he hesitated for a moment in front of the arched doorway. Looming above him were stone walls; solid buttresses and a castellated tower that made the building look more like a fortress. On his right side stood a Celtic cross and around its base were carved some words that were illegible through the crusts of yellow lichen. A yew tree in the far corner formed a silhouette of branching wings like that of a bird of prey. Between its feathers could be seen the dark clouds that brooded over the horizon. There was a shifting in the air, a gathering of notes; a single chime perhaps, but not quite. He knew about the legend of the belfry.

As a child, in the school holidays, he would go down to the quayside with scraps of bacon that he had filched from the kitchen. He hooked them on the end of a line and threw them over the side of the pier. It was there that he met the men who darned their nets, their weathered faces folded in as they waited for the tide to turn. On days when a sea mist crept over the shore he noticed that their faces turned towards the church on the hill. He wondered why they did this and Old Sam hesitated as he pulled the pipe from his mouth before he told him the terrible tale.

"And they'll be back, boy" he said. "You mark my words. When that church bell rings, you run boy, run for your life."

Aldwyn was frightened by what the old man had told him and could not sleep for several nights afterwards. But that was when he was a child. As far as Aldwyn knew there was nobody who could remember a time when the bell had rung out. In any case, the rope was too short for an ordinary person to reach it and it was slung over the wooden flag pole where the mice had gnawed it and used the hemp fibres to line their nests.

He was more cynical as a grown up and he believed that the tale had only been revived to entertain the visitors. It added a touch of mystery to the twilight tours. No doubt Gerry from The Slubbers thought it a great ruse as he led the tourists through a maze of snickets and ginnels, all the while telling them ghoulish tales. By the time they reached the steep path to the church the sun had usually gone down beyond the far hills and it was only by the light of his flame torch that they could see the winged shadows of bats swooping and skittering over their heads. They gladly returned to the comfort of the pub.

Now, Aldwyn stood facing the riveted door, waiting for the familiar sound of the key as it located into the mechanism. His movements were methodical as if performing a sacred ritual. Indeed, he took his job as Keeper of Antiquities very seriously. He didn't consider that the word Caretaker properly described his role. As he entered the church he could hear the creak of the weather vane on the roof.

From behind the door, a broom fell and clattered onto the floor, its wooden handle echoed on the stone flags. He reached along the wall for a switch and a flickering low light filled the entrance. Once he'd adjusted to the gloom he moved forward, his fingers trailing the familiar outline of the fossilised ichsyosaurus. It had been excavated from the shale beach by a famous palaeontologist in the 1970's and for a while it had seemed that the eyes of the world were on their village. It had been necessary to them to find a home for the great fish, hence, the transformation from church to museum. It had become a well known centre for the study and research of local history, receiving donations of artefacts and old documents.

In fact, an old parchment manuscript was presently being translated into modern English. It was a saga documenting

118

a raid on the village by a Viking called Nord Axehead. The tale was one of horrific murder, mutilation, rape and the burning down of the whole settlement. Details were not spared, if anything, they were lingered upon until every drop of spilled blood had been accounted for.

Aldwyn shivered when he saw the curled corner of the document in its glass case. He shivered as he made his way toward the main exhibition but everything seemed to be in order. The previous day, a class of seven year olds from St Bede's had visited for a History Experience Day and he had half expected to be greeted with an untidy scattering of paper cuttings and unsheathed felt pens.

Further on Aldwyn approached the nave, the section that had been designated *The Anglo Saxon Village*. Here was a cross-section of a granary, a forge and a family home with lifelike models frozen in the performance of their daily tasks. A waxen blacksmith, anvil in hand, was at his usual place by the smithy fire where the rotating lights were reflected in moving shadows on the wall behind. Aldwyn sniffed the air and thought he detected a wisp of smoke. It was amazing what the mind could imagine although when he thought about it, it was more likely to be coming from someone's garden bonfire. It was the time of year for collecting up the fallen leaves.

As he stood there he could hear that outside the church walls the wind was increasing steadily. The door behind him batted open and shut again. He felt the cold air, so cold as if it had come from the icy north. It seemed to be circling around the graveyard now, around and around, spiralling around the headstones. He thought of the flowers that had been placed in the holed containers at the head of each grave, how the petals would be scattered and flung over the cliff edge.

He was at the forge door and Aldwyn could look

through to the village huts beyond. They were being attacked by a band of Viking marauders who had thrown their orange painted torches at a thatched roof. He reminded himself that it was not real fire, nor were they real Vikings. It was a reconstruction, to demonstrate how it would have looked back then.

He thought it was all rather unnecessary. Somebody must have decided to play a few tricks by coming to the museum at night and changing the scene from one of peaceful rustic employment to one of dreadful destruction.

The wind outside had gained speed and was lurching like a dervish from church to yew and back, butting against the ancient walls. Clods of soil were snatched from the ground and lobbed against the stained glass windows, falling back to the ground in heavy pats. The noise alarmed Aldwyn and as he looked up the windows quivered so much he thought they might actually be blown inwards. Even the pigment seemed to be parting from the glass.

At his feet were scattered a dozen or so replica chickens, baskets were spilled, pails of liquid upturned, their contents staining the floor. He heard a woman's scream and the whinnying of a horse. It was all very realistic. The museum staff must have worked hard to illustrate such a full sensory experience.

He shivered as hailstones pummelled the windows. Then the wind stopped as suddenly as it had begun and the vacuum of silence was filled with a blood curdling bellow. At the same time, the large bell tilted in the belfry, clanking over and over in unmelodic discord.

Standing by the village well was a man. He wore a horned helmet, an axe held aloft with both hands. The whites of his eyes could be seen around the circumference of each iris. His toothless mouth was opened wide in a bloody grimace. He was so

120

life like that for a moment Aldwyn flinched when the axe came down.

The scene around him reeled until his eyes focussed on a clasp that held the man's cloak. As he studied the detail he thought that something was wrong. It was made of brass and engraved with Celtic knots. The model dresser had simply made a mistake but it seemed incongruous with the rest of the meticulously created scene. Perhaps it had been placed there to demonstrate that such an item would have been prized by the invaders. So clever, these museum curators, he thought.

The noise from the bell was very distracting but he steadied himself long enough to notice the man's ankle boots. No doubt the dark blotches on the leather were to represent the bloodstains typical of that on a warrior's footwear after a good day's slaying.

He blinked; his sight was tinted pink. To his surprise he could taste something familiar and metallic on his tongue. He thought of the rare steak he had eaten a few days before. Yes, it was the taste of blood, but this blood had trickled down his face from the open wound in his head. It was his blood. Old Sam's word came back to him now but he could no longer run. As he hit the ground, the bell stopped its awful clanging.

Apple Tree

Through the bay window she can see them. They are seated elbow to elbow around a circular table. Light spirals down from a central lamp; shadows beyond. Five places are laid out on the table. Four people are present; a model family of a mother, a father and two boys. They look like they are twins. All are perfectly framed within the window, heads close, teeth neat within their smiles; tinkling conversation arches around them, nudging, embracing; knitting them together. There is an echo of scraping knives on plates and then an abrupt clink. A replete belch is followed by the reprimanding voice of Mother. She is collecting up the plates, including the clean one that sits in front of the empty chair. She picks at loose crumbs on the table's surface, looks pointedly at the feet that press against the leg of the table tilting a chair at a dangerous angle.

It is an ordinary, contented, domestic scene. Even the apple pie sits plump and perfect at the centre of the table, its golden crust crowned with delicate pastry leaves; sweet steam rising from the beak of the china blackbird. The custard is smooth and creamy and soon the children's pink cheeks have yellow smears. The humming conversation rises up and up until the room is bursting. The window frame shakes as the door is thrown open and the children come running into the garden, bullish and buoyant.

"Be very careful," commands Mother.

"Do as your mother says." These words come from a deeper voice.

The family is a lasso handed between the hands of Mother and Father; an invisible rope that encircles the children, draws them in, and lets them out little by little.

The boys go straight to the apple tree. One climbs the

rope ladder; the other grabs the bottom rung and shakes it hard. The climber is yelling but soon finds a purchase for one foot. He swings himself up onto the platform, picks up an apple and throws it over the edge. It is a windfall; gone yellow, partly brown with white specks of ferment. It lands a bull's eye on its target and as it splits the sweet cider goo covers the back of the other boy's head.

Unseen by either boy, a girl is curling her top lip in disgust. She walks to the other side of the garden where the dying herbaceous flowers are frayed and toughened with play. She sinks onto a sheaf of montbretia. It forms a nest around her and hidden from the others she opens a book and begins to read. It is old and leather bound; its gold edged pages drop their powdered glitter. Her red hair floats amongst the flower heads as tiny spiders climb around the fine strands and ants traverse her freckled ankles.

Her eyes close.

She dreams that she knows of a house in a place she cannot see. It is hidden behind a high stone wall. She feels her way along the stones beneath a curtain of ivy until she finds a door. The latch has turned brittle and orange with rust. Within the splintered wood is an empty knothole. Peering through, she sees an eye looking back at her. A strand of hair falls in front of it. The watcher's hair is also red. She lifts her hand as if to reach out and push it clear of the eye but as it winks, she blinks awake into the sunlight and flicks away the insect whose fine proboscis tickles her cheek.

It was only a year ago when the moon was high and she woke in her own bed. A voice was echoing her name. The familiar tones had a sweetness that drew her name vowel over vowel. Pulling back the curtain she could see the apple tree, its branches were still, not a leaf moved. The surrounding grass was an unfurled roll of silver satin. She shivered and firmly closed the curtains. Then she slipped back beneath the covers.

In the morning her ironed clothes were on the chair, their symmetrical creases inviting her to swim her arms up and out between their straight lines. The aroma of toast drew her down the stairs.

"Sleep well, darling?" Mother asked.

"I kept dreaming and I was afraid," she replied. "I heard a voice calling my name."

"Just a dream," Mother said.

But the following night it happened again. This time she felt a pull on her arms and she rose out of sleep to see the stars winking in the darkness. Once again she was sure that she heard her name being called. It was the same voice as before, rich and familiar. She thought her dreams must be carried on the wisps of cloud that passed through the night sky. She fell into a fitful sleep and woke up in the daylight to find a chanting blackbird perched at the top of the apple tree. He sang the same song over and over. It upset her.

"Oh, there you are. You slept well. Were you making up for the night before?" Mother said wrapping her arms around her daughter.

As she lifted a spoonful of cereal to her lips the girl looked out at the garden. It was a dull autumn day; the greens were dark grey and the branches of the tree were almost black. Only the heads of the late crocosmia gave the garden any colour. The few leaves on the apple tree were limp and tossed lifelessly this way and that in the breeze. An apple hung from one of the higher branches. It fascinated her; the way that it caught the light it seemed as if it were made of silver.

Outside, she stretched up but it was just out of reach. She ran and leapt as high as she could. Determined, she climbed up the ladder. It swung out as she pushed her feet into the rungs. Her arms stretched, their muscles burned with the effort. From the platform she looked down, faltered and wavering like a falling leaf she glided down and down into the black ground.

Now, she looks over to the house. She can see right inside. Her father enters the kitchen with her brothers who carry boots and kit bags. The bathroom light is switched on and the hissing sound of the boiler can be heard as the bath taps run. Aunty is at the kitchen sink filling the kettle and talking to Father. He sits at the table, head in hands. He nods from side to side at something that Aunty is saying. She places a cup in front of him, puts a hand on his shoulder and turns her back to the window. Mother is in the upstairs hallway, her arms reach above the coloured glass lights. Very slowly she pulls blankets from a top cupboard.

The girl tries to call out, to tell them she loves them all; that she is still with them even though they cannot see her. All is quiet until the girl hears her name being called. But it is not her mother's voice; it is the sound of the rustling leaves in the apple tree.

Tweed

You are surprised by the weight of the casket. Only a week ago her hand was like a bird's feather, fine bones holding the slight wing of flesh that you stroked and stroked until she fell asleep. Now your shopping bag is bulging, straining at the seams; its handles bite into your hand.

"All aboard the magic bus," the conductor says, winking.

You feel as if you have been nudged into an empty seat. The flowers are next to you, their yellow heads quiver with the vibration of the burring engine.

The bell rings and the bus stops, this time to let on an elderly woman. The conductor knows her name and helps her aboard. With a flourish, he offers her an arm, one eyebrow raised, as if requesting the next dance. She sits with you. She is wearing a winter coat, blue and cream tweed.

You look with envy at the stairs. You want to go up there but you are afraid of the jolting and lurching of the bus. Up above it is a different world; a place where you can look down at the striped awnings over the shop fronts and imagine how you could jump and bounce onto the canvas. There are windows of mute rectangles, empty rooms, floors cracked with curling linoleum, faded strips, sun streaked curtains, guarded privacy. Sometimes you pass the kitchens of cafes where people stand at sinks wearing aprons or hairnets, filling kettles, emptying pans, lifting great pots. Others lean out of open windows, lit cigarettes hang off their limp wrists as smoke rings rise to join the clouds. There are faded Formica tables, boxes of cereal with red cockerel combs, crooked sofas that slope on missing wheels, odd shaped succulents thirsting on windowsills, and fingers of bolting cheese plants that splay the panes of glass like waving hands.

But today, you are downstairs and there is little to feed your curiosity. You swing out your feet. Underfoot, the floor is littered with old tickets. With the toe end of your shoes you kick the paper ribbons up towards the cushioned bottom of the seat in front. Then you lean forward, grasp the rail and taste its sweet metal in your mouth. In front of you is the back of a head. You are entranced by each shiny bristle that stands proud of the wrinkled neck. You are reminded of the antimacassars at Gran's house, their stained hollows edged in lace and you wonder whether, now, they adorn some other winged chairs.

Through the windows the familiar route unfurls and you recognise the people who wait at the bus stops, always the same day of the week, the same time; the same place. Soon they are clattering along the aisle, flinging themselves into seats just as the clutch is beginning to bite. There are the stragglers, the young ones who have run for the bus, hurling themselves onto the platform, clattering up the stairs, drumming their feet above the driver's cab.

As the bus lifts over the rise of the bridge the conductor announces, 'Swan Lake,' the first word lengthening like the neck of a swan.

You look through the balustrades of the bridge to the flat surface of the river. It is running slowly today, almost stilled in the midday sun. The glare of the reflection makes it shine like an ice rink. You think you can see dancers skating on the skin surface, pirouetting, circling and gliding until the ghostly ballerinas are swallowed by the big fish; their top lips enveloping, drawing in the unfiltered river air.

The bus sways and feel the tautness of her arm next to you, the hand firmly fixed on the bar in front.

"Do try and sit still," says the woman next to you.

She does not look at you. Her lips are taut, a perfect arc.

128

'Fares please,' says the conductor from under a half cocked peak.

You hand over the change and when he gives you the ticket, he winks.

"Give us a smile, love."

You roll the ticket between your fingers and the leak of the ink is purple and fresh. You wipe it on your clothes. You keep rolling until the ticket forms a pipe and hold it up to your eye, fixing it onto the dark mole of the neck in front. A perfect fit.

You are nearly right the way across town and it must be time to press the bell. You allow the tension in your thumb to release. You stand up once when the driver has pressed on the brakes and then you are shuffling towards the open back of the bus in a line with all the others. There you are, enjoying the sliding soles of your patent shoes. The conductor is leering and then he makes his final announcement.

"Valley of Death,' he grins. 'All change."

From the bunch of flowers, a single head of chrysanthemum has fallen. You bend to pick it up but you are urged along by the other passengers. You watch as one by one each yellow petal is caught under the sole of a black brogue, released in ones and twos with each forward step. They remain on the floor of the bus, flattened and bruised while the aroma of crushed chrysanthemum pervades the air.

You stand by the curb of the pavement, coughing and blinking through the acrid fumes of the departing bus. There is no other traffic but she is holding your hand. Everywhere is silent and then you hear the craw of a single crow from the high branches of a tree on the other side of the road.

The street is wide and the tarmac is hot beneath your feet. On the other side, the big gates are flanked on either side by stone pillars. The latch is hot under your hand where the black paint has bubbled in the sun.

Now you have entered a garden of endless rows. You are walking behind her now and she has let go of your hand. You search amongst the rows and rows of stones for the place.

When you find it, you kneel by the cold hearth, run your fingers along the polished surface of the granite and feel the coolness of the silver lettering. You shake the contents of the casket onto the gravel and say a prayer as you mix the ashes and ashes, the dust and dust. Now they are together.

The rumble of the bus comes from beyond the railings. You feel panic. You cannot leave yet, not until you have seen her. You know she is here somewhere. As you walk along the lines of headstones you turn and scan the rows of black marble, grey plinths, white pillars, stone crosses, the one that is marked by a mere rock.

You must not stay for long in the 'Valley of Death'. You hurry towards the bus but you look back one more time and then you see her. She is smiling and as she turns you see the arc of a wing as she slips behind a great carved stone.

"Come along, Madam. Last bus today," says the conductor. "You don't want to be left here, do you?"

He laughs. Then he holds out his hand and grasps your sleeve of blue and cream tweed.

The Colour of Glass

Nan is the only Original left. Many have forgotten the bravery of the young woman who saved the lives of several people in the wake of the devastation caused by the Red Moon. Now they see only an old woman working at a furnace, the plait of grey hair looped around her head, cheeks mottled cherry red in the heat. She blows and wields the molten glass, twirling the glowing poker, holding it up and beating it down onto the marble slab, bending the treacle, forming spouts, lips, handles, loops. She nips and tweezes until she is content with her vision of transparency. Every shelf is full, three deep with lamps and goblets and jugs and bottles and even a bowl of glass eye balls. Her work is her life but her life began in another world. The items she makes no longer have a practical use. Now, there are synthesised materials, so easily produced and cheaply too. They can be moulded into any form that is required.

There are some who still enjoy the beauty of glass objects but they do not speak of it. There is nothing to be gained from indulging in visual satisfaction, they are told, and that it is an outdated concept from an old world when people believed in something called the imagination, an intangible thing that cannot be proved, and therefore, does not exist. Such beliefs are dangerous in this new world and Nan has been indulged for long enough. Today, a Council meeting has been scheduled. An important decision is to be made, one that has not been taken before: to decide a person's fate, in this case, Nan's.

Sula is the youngest and the only woman present. The Board are keen to be seen to acknowledge the views of the young adults they purportedly represent. The route to becoming a representative for any sector has become more difficult with the passing of new laws. In fact, it is a process so cumbersome and longwinded that most do not attempt it.

Sula has been fast tracked along the system because the Elders believe she is the least troublesome of her generation but that she holds the trust of her fellows. Consequently, she has been assigned the role of Single Speaker. This means that she is allowed to express her opinion once, and once only. She is prohibited from repeating herself, unlike the others, who do so all of the time. If she tries to expand her point, the elders will be quick to prevent her from continuing. Today, she has not yet spoken. She has an idea but it must wait until after the midsession break. It involves a visit to a filing cabinet in the restricted area of the Lower Hall.

Third generation Orbisher, Jonti P, is seated at the boardroom table where the shiny surface reflects the piles of legal papers, the evidence for the case. The light from the window has draped a pearly sheen over the room and the deep shadows accentuate the features of those present. Jonti's elbows are propped on the table and he chews his tongue as he twirls a lock of blond hair. Morality and mortality do not interest him. He would prefer to be at his work in the lab amongst the test tubes and Petri dishes than to sit around a table discussing human resource levels. At least experiments are methodical, they have specific aims, they have hypothesise that can be verified, falsified, validated. Here, there are no absolutes, no obvious conclusions.

He looks across at Sula. With her glasses balanced on her head, her hair is held back, revealing the curve of her ears, the cut of her cheekbone. She notices him and momentarily flicks her eyes in his direction but at that moment she is more interested in what is being said by Marlo.

Marlo's dark sideburns are flecked with silver, his fingers tap on the table as he speaks.

"Nan is the bravest person I have ever known," he is

saying. "She saved so many when the Red Moon came.

There is a general mumbling of agreement from the others in the room.

"She swam across a raging river carrying the children on her back," his voice starts to break and he drifts, swallowing his words. He knows that any decision that is contrary to the motion must be unanimous.

Marlo's father had been one of the Originals and suffered greatly once he had arrived on Orbish, complaining relentlessly that he could not breathe, that there was never enough air in the atmosphere. Really, the oxygen levels were perfectly adequate for human habitation but it was not what he was used to; the air did not buffet or swirl around like the winds from the north and the west that blew across the mountains of his early life.

Seventy years have passed since the Red Moon fell into the elliptical arc of the Earth. It had come as a surprise when the collision happened and the results were completely unexpected and unlike any predictions that had been calculated by the scientists. There were no explosions, no great meteor showers or interplanetary displays, no showy exhibitions of floating rock. In fact it had been remarkably quiet, just the faint hiss of falling fireworks; and then, complete silence. But although the debris was invisible, the Earth's elements had been transformed in a way that could not have been imagined or presupposed; splitting each cell into many parts, cross oscillating through every component. It was very discombobulating. Before long, the resulting instability caused the mountains to divide, producing shifts and rifts, fragmenting rock, splitting valleys. Shuddering earthquakes arose from the core and fresh volcanoes spat wrathful molten fire which in turn caused thousands of hectares of impenetrable steam. The world became a place of impossible divides.

In their panic, people had grabbed hold of anything they could: a child, a suitcase, a length of rope, a tablecloth, an egg. Even a filing cabinet of old documents had made its way with them. As an enormous cloud drifted towards them it rested on the side of a hill and several people ran towards it just as it started to crystallise. The exterior quickly formed into a crust, the vital nutrients stabilized, and a patch of land became encapsulated. Inside was a perfect and habitable miniature world. This pod of humans and various other life forms; animal, vegetable and mineral, were the useful beginnings of the establishment of the new colony. They named this new world Orbish because it was round like an orb, but; not quite.

They found the means to everything they needed: food from the micro cultures in the spores of lichen, water from internal cloud evaporation; chambers for shelter. The latter were at first formed from woven materials that eventually they learned to synthesise and form moulded pods for desks, chairs, beds, plates, beakers; anything of practical use albeit of a functional kind. Pods were built that fitted into the curves of the clouds. The only drawback was that everything was the same colour, the colour of cloud.

They worked hard and if ever there was a dispute it was always Nan they called on to arbitrate, but now, all these years later, poor Nan's time is up. She is at the 'morphus point' and today the Committee meets to decide her 'date'. Although her medication is easy to manufacture in the Orbish Laboratories, there are signs (to some) that Nan's condition is no longer responding. There has been evidence of melted glass appearing in places where it should not be, distorting, warping and reflecting mirrored images of the inhabitants. Nan, like everyone else on Orbish, has signed The Contract and the purpose of today's meeting is to invoke it.

Yerek, as usual, is in opposition to everything Marlo says. He has already made it clear that there is no question in his mind. Nan is of no use to them, they have carried her for long enough. She simply represents a false nostalgia for an old world. He is interested in the present and the future, and in particular, his own future.

"We have limited resources as it is," he argues. "We don't even know how long Orbish can sustain us."

"I am not talking about numbers and figures here," Marlo says, looking irritated.

"I am talking about humanity, something we could lose altogether if we are not careful."

"What use is humanity when before long there will be no humans left," Yerek's lip curls in disdain as he mutters under his breath, "or at least just a few of us."

"So that's it, is it?" Marlo is indignant.

His voice is strengthened with anger.

"Let's be clear shall we?" he continues. "What we are talking about is the care we show for our elderly, and we..." Marlo points his finger at each of them around the table, "...are deciding whether we think Nan should live or die."

Sula has struggled and at times has felt great despair; only last year she came to the conclusion that their way of life was futile and pointless. She spent a month in her chamber, hardly coming out to eat or drink and never speaking to anyone. Her friends were worried and begged Nan to help

"It is for you," Nan said presenting Sula with a curved blue vase. "It is the colour of the sky and one day I hope you will see it."

Sula had heard about the skies of azure, sapphire and the indigo nights and the sunsets with their rays of rose and orange and other colours that she could only begin to imagine. She had grown up in a grey white cloud but when she held up the glass vase and saw the shifting beams glancing off the walls in rainbows; she saw hope.

"It is the most beautiful thing ever!" she exclaimed.

Nan had once been apprenticed to a glassblower, a craftswoman of the ancient art and once on Orbish; she was keen to set up a furnace. The only source of raw material was the crumbly grey sand and consequently the objects she made were of no practical use. Nevertheless, many enjoyed their curves and interesting textures, and the way the glass held on to the bubbles, trapping them in a translucent world. At first they were used for ceremonies, decorations, chimes, as ritual chalices but these events were soon banned. The Board members complained that it was all witchcraft; a hangover from a backward culture. Tensions ran so high that a new law was passed by the Pragmatic Council:

Point 2:1   *Activities deemed to be not in the interest of the practical furtherance of the community will no longer be tolerated. All items of an aesthetic nature will be confiscated and the purveyor or owner of such items will be punished.*

The punishment was not specified and in any case nobody was ever prosecuted. It was more of a warning shot to be fired over the boughs of the Orbish public at times of unrest. Now, there was a malaise spreading through the population. It was as if people were bored with survival; as if maintaining the practical details of living was no longer enough. Sula believes that the answer lies in Nan's knowledge but she will have to convince

136

the Board.

It is the mid session break and all have left the room except Jonti and Sula.

"Can we take our break together?" he asks.

Sula hesitates.

"Ok, but I have some reading to do before this afternoon's session," she says. "I'll meet you back at my pod. I just need to check something out."

He is standing at her door with a bottle of Zubajuice when she arrives. Once inside she puts the papers face down onto the table.

"Busy day today so far," he comments. "We'll never get through the agenda at this rate."

"Mmm..." Sula seems distracted.

He is smiling. Of course, she knows that he knows that she purposefully turned over the papers but she must be ready for his arguments. He leans in towards her and as she puts a hand up to stop him, a draught riffles through the papers and they slip onto the floor. They both watch as one sheet curls over revealing its printed side.

'Paragraph 3B Creation and the Appreciation of Beauty.'

"What the...?"

His face is flushed, his eyes darkening as if a live animal has come between them, one that means to tear them apart.

Sula grabs the paper.

"Don't say anything," she commands.

"But where the hell did you get that?" he whispers.

"It's all in the archives – if you know where to look."

"Sula, you know all that stuff is forbidden, you shouldn't even be there."

"Look, I only have the one chance," she pleads. "I need to save Nan."

"I just don't understand why you care so much for the old lady." He sounds genuinely puzzled.

"I know you don't understand," she says slowly and she takes a deep breath before she explains it to him.

He becomes very quiet.

"OK," he says, eventually, "What is it you want from me? You heard what I said at the meeting. They'll know something's going on if I vote against the motion now."

"I want you to really understand," she says.

Sula pulls the cork on the Zubajuice and pours it into two long stemmed glasses. She lifts one to the light allowing the purple and rose tints to shimmer as the bubbles leap over the rim. Jonti sighs. She passes the glass to him and as he lifts it to his lips, she knows she has gained his vote.

Erthenta

Only those who dwell in caves can really understand. When the surface is a barren dry desert and the sun burns on and on, there is nowhere else to go. The caves becomes your world, your home, your street, your back yard; your life. No darkness enters from above; there is none, not since the final spin of the Earth on its axel nearly a century before. This is the place they call Erthenta. Once you experience the lure of the silence, the calling of the calm, the cool air caressing the flesh of your face, you will never again want to resurface.

Elsina has lived here for twenty year-longs. The dark soil and shadowed rock beneath the burnt crust of Earth is her homeland. She ventures to the surface only long enough to seek out the scorched creatures that provide the community with a little cooked protein. At least there is a steady supply of water in the under layer where the streams ooze from the mountains of ice on the other side of the planet. Channelled, there is enough to quench the thirst of all Erthentans before it is evaporated by the surface heat, turning liquid to steam. Special midway caves have been set aside for the steam rooms where people can go after their day's labours to sink their weary flesh into the vivifying banks of mud, to cleanse in the rich mineral pools and sup from the pure springs.

They all believe their true home, the place of their origin, is at the centre of the Earth. It is a place they all aspire to visit at least once in their lives, to meditate at the holy shrine of Shala, to relieve their troubles, to submit their prayers, to feel the embrace of the inner void. But the path to the centre is known to be hazardous, crumbling with every rumble, splitting with each quake of the endlessly shifting tectonic plates. Those who make it back speak of the haunting sounds, the creaking of rock that can be more terrifying than even the scorching winds or the tongues of searing fire that abound the surface.

Elsina lives with her partner, Elk. They plan to make their pilgrimage in sixty day-longs when their soon-to-be-born child will be past the dangers of the firstling months. To take a baby to the womb of the Earth is deemed the highest honour a parent can bestow upon their child. It is believed that the soul from that time will be protected by Shala, the Spirit of Inner Earth. Most are not brave enough to attempt the dangerous journey as so few survive the gauntlet of the dark chambers, the twisting corridors and the rock falls, to return unscathed.

On this night, as on every other, Elsina has left her base at the beginning of sleep time and she will return by first wake. She must check that all the workforce have adhered to the safety measures. The work is dangerous: digging, clearing passageways, forging new routes, building props to reinforce the old. It is the Undergangers job to drill chains of holes where there are no natural inlets and insert the long hollow solar pipes. Once they have light they can then penetrate deeper towards the centre of the Earth. It is a dangerous mission and a single slip can result in immediate burial, alive.

It is not long before Elsina meets an Undergang, their ochre faces are weary but there is lightness about them, unusual after a day of heavy and tedious graft. She checks her time log. They have worked for longer than their allocated shift and they are unusually animated tonight, chatting amongst themselves, unlike the exhausted silence that generally greets her. Their picks are slung over their shoulders, rivulets of sweat stream the contours of their faces but despite their fatigue they are whistling and the light from a solar pipe catches the whites of their teeth, Elsina can see they are smiling.

"You are very late tonight. Is everything all right?" Elsina asks.

"We have made a breakthrough," says Carla, whose dark eyes are rimmed with white. "See for yourself – Tunnel 59, Southside." She winks. "There's a treat in store for you."

"I'll look forward to that," Elsina replies.

She wonders if they have found another geode. The last one proved to be made of black crystal, its power so great—far more that its weight times the gravitational pull—that it had bored its way through several meters of solid bedrock. It must have arrived during the final meteor shower of the last century when most of the surface population were annihilated. The force of the shower was so powerful that it caused the planet to halt, interrupting its trajectory and knocking it from its axis.

This black geode was buried in the ground, undiscovered for decades until the Undergangers had started work on the new passageways project. They suddenly came to a halt, met by an impenetrable wall. Then, unexpectedly, just as they were about to give up, they burst through the hard casing of a geode. Once the shell had been broached and a new light channel fixed in place they found that they were standing inside a glittering gemstone the size of the largest of the refectory caverns.

Her job as Network Coordinator means that she must be constantly aware of any changes or amendments to the job specifications, plus she must have a full understanding of the system, keeping up to date with new tunnels and acting as Consultant for each and every new link from its planning stage to its realisation. She has a good knowledge of all the subways, as if they are the veins and arteries that flow and ebb around her own body; a sub world map that is imprinted on her mind. She can navigate through the ginnels of the clustered chambers when the main arterials are at their busiest, she can be a compass just like the one carried by her grandfather (whose confidence in the Core

Pole never faltered). At the end of each day she treads each and every route, checking for threats of subsidence. Someone is walking ahead of her now, slowly, bumping from sidewall to sidewall. She puts one hand on the shoulder and a girl's face turns towards her, eyes open but opaque—the eyes of a sleepwalker.

"Come, let me take you home," Elsina says and gently leads her towards the chambered area just as the girl's mother rushes towards them, embracing the girl.

"She is found!" she exclaims. "All praise to Shala".

Further along, the others are sleeping in the silence. Just like breathing, the silence of the dark is their inhalation, the oxygen of their well being. There is never a day break; a dawn chorus, a creeping grey light to absorb the dark, just an instinctual itch that stirs them, synchronising their waking and sleeping hours. The rhythm of the breathing sleepers begins to lull her away from her own thoughts into a peaceful state. Elsina sinks into an alcove where there is a resting ledge. She yawns.

"Let me take your watch tonight," Elk had said to her earlier that evening.

"It's ok," she had replied, "I must continue for as long as I am able."

"But there is darkness beneath your eyes, a heaviness..."

"That maybe so," she interjected, "but my strength holds. I will get bored if I do not work."

Elsina rubs the small of her back and sets off through the dimly lit passages. She knows that she is in danger of losing her focus, her energy is low. She must keep her mind alert. She is nearing her 'long resting' time and she cannot wait to hold her newborn, to see its face, its tiny hands. There have been no new babies for a generation and many people are holding Elsina in the light of their minds. She represents the future for them all; their hopes enshrined in the roundness of her abdomen.

She rubs her belly to sooth the twitching form beneath her taut skin and as she does her mind wanders over the delicious moments of their sleep time. She likes it when Elk traces the darkening thread of her linea nigra, breaking off to kiss the slight movements on either side; and when they sleep, their naked bodies lay curled as one, her face pressed into the earthy scents, her belly nudging between them.

As she rounds the corner something moves, a shape, amorphous, indefinable, and it is slipping, slithering down the cave wall. She rubs her eyes and touches the walls of the passageway on her left and then her right. Both are solid. She checks her coordinates. She is at the newly mined place. She is afraid that her fatigue has slipped her guard, that she will be prey to the vibes that are believed to lurk in the cavities waiting for the moment of their release. There are many rumours.

She yearns for Elk. How she wishes she had agreed that tonight they would stay together. Again, she thinks about their love making and remembers that moment, the one when she opened up and felt the seed planting itself within her. It was like a pain; an insistent niggle that carried on for several days. She knew that it was a new life but at first she said nothing, determined to enjoy her secret alone, hugging it with her whole being. Now that same life is almost ready to emerge. Already she can hear its voice; a small, quiet voice that broaches the divide of flesh.

"Beware," it whispers.

She shivers with the vibration of the sound. It is like a ripple across a lake. She stops and she stands still, not breathing, all conscious of her surroundings. She must control her mind, analyse the situation, she must not be drawn into the tiny world that awaits her; not yet. But she must take heed. There is very little that can harm her here, the shadows are just that, shadows; and even if they aren't they have no reason to haunt her. But she is uneasy. A light flickers.

Slap.

She is hit on the back.

"Ow!" she exclaims and turns around.

On the ground is a beached Carcomite, its legs wavering in the air. It must have slipped and fallen several hundred feet or more to reach these caves and now it is weak; exhausted by the way it feebly scrambles, straddle backed on the floor, circling on the bowl of its shell.

Beached on its back, Elsina knows that it is helpless. She even feels sympathy for it but not for long. The poison from the hardened glands of these cretaceous creatures is enough to kill or at best, paralyse a person. She pulls out her Carcafork and without hesitation she stabs through the solar plexus and watches as the blue light fades. She sighs. The day shift must have missed this one. As dangerous as they are, they are stupid creatures with no sense of self preservation and fearless when it comes to humans who can simply finish them off with a single stab. She lifts it by its tail and slings it into her backpack.

The path ahead of her slopes downwards as she enters the district of Southside. Here are the salting lakes where all their food is taken and preserved. It is a job that they all share; like washing their clothes in the icy rivers or weaving the carriers for the Undergangs to use when they are removing newly dug out rock. Here, they roll the pieces of creature meat in the brine at the edge of the lakes. Then they are stored in barrels, carved out from the branchless trunks that lay around on the surface. These gnarled growths survive but are stunted in the extreme temperatures. Only by huddling around the deep set light shafts can they thrive. Their bark is thick around the slow growing wood but inside they are succulent.

Here the cave rock is grey. All around, the walls are dripping with condensation, underfoot it is slippery from the mulch of leaves dropped by the spindle trees. It is cooler here but the steam still rises and swirls.

"Elsina! Have you heard the news?" It is Jarrish, the apothecary's apprentice coming towards her in the mist.

"Hi Jarrish, how goes it today? Whoa..."

Jarrish catches hold of her arm before she slips to the floor.

"You must be careful. Hold onto this barrel for a moment, catch your breath and then I will show you something."

"Is it about Tunnel 59?" Elsina remembers the elation of the Undergangers. "I have heard that something has been found but I don't know any more than that."

"Come on. I shouldn't really but everyone's gone home now."

His pale face is caught in the green shaft light giving him a strange drained look. The lack of solar had taken its toll. She follows him past the powdering tables where the grounding processes take place; the dried extractions are used as medicinal compounds and applied for many ailments. The proboscises of dead Carcomites lay in rows on a bench in readiness. Nothing is wasted. Even the horny shells, the hardest material found below ground can be attached to long bone handles and used as spades by the Undergangers. The eyes, like black pearls, gleam in their bowls. They are prized and used to embellish their clothes, decorating both waistbands and shoulder pads.

Tunnel 59 is straight ahead of them now. It had been closed while work is in progress. Elsina can see where the slippage has occurred. To the left of the entrance is a crack in the wall, an opening large enough to squeeze through.

"Are you sure it's safe?" she asks Jarrish.

"I've been through it several times today and it seems fine," he replies.

There is a broadening beyond the narrow entrance that opens out into a chamber, nothing particularly unusual in that. The temperature is steady, not too hot, nor too cold. She stands back for a moment to adjust her eyes to the gloom.

"Well, it's always good to find new caverns," Elsina can see no point in staying any longer. "I suppose they will be working on a light shaft tomorrow."

Jarresh is behind her and strikes a flame, lighting up a hand torch.

"Look," he said pointing to the far wall of the chamber.

She does not see it at first and even then she feels annoyed at the time she has already wasted. Her shift will never end at this rate. Then she sees it, the opening with the light coming from beyond. But where does it come from? No shaft has yet been built but there is a colour, mauve and purple—an amethyst glow. The passageway is lined with lilac crystals that give off a light of their own. It is not a cave but a passageway that carries on for as far as the eye can see.

"Have you been any further?" she asks Jarrish.

"I have," he replies. "I have walked for half a day and there is no sign of it ending. I believe it is a passageway to the centre of the Earth."

The twinge of the daybreak alarm is beginning to pulse in her head. She knows she must return. Now she cannot get there fast enough, exhilarated by what she has seen. She must tell Elk about the new tunnel. They will go there together with their newborn. They will take their child along the amethyst path to the centre of the Earth to receive its perpetual blessing.

With renewed energy, Elsina slips lithely through the

146

snickets, steals unseen into the fast lanes. The heat is increasing as she approaches the mid surface area. The white light from the blazing sun is so fierce that the heat is seeping ever quicker into the deepest places through the narrowest funnels. Never dark, the shafts of light plunge in from the natural openings and gullies and fill the hallways with a radiant pulse.

Elsina weaves through tunnels instinctively turning, crossing, and zigzagging until she is nearly at the place where Elk sleeps. She hurries, she cannot wait. They must make plans. She knows that they are only safe in the shallow hollows for a little while longer. It cannot be long before the ever increasing heat will burn them all to cinders. They have no option while the Earth is imprisoned by the Sun Star's fire.

Swarm

Flicking their lithe rudders they spit beads of water into Maysu's face. She laughs and splutters before diving down again.

"Wingfish are so beautiful!" she says to her father afterwards. Father merely frowns.

"Kiri quar kiri!" calls Maysu.

She is the youngest Watterishi and the fish respond to her by twisting up in a playful fountain. The Wingfish are speckled in a rainbow of colours. Such beauty is unusual in the world of Watterish; the place where grey skies and green brown land merge into a khaki camouflage.

Brushing off the tiny button scales from her jacket Father gives a loud bellow.

The fish turn, shift as one and head toward the centre of the lake. The Wingfish are an enigma to him but he knows they understand him by the tone of his voice.

"That's it for today," he says.

"Shouldn't we leave some for the fish?" Maysu asks, glancing at their nets full of the Gringrow garlands

"Huh," Father scoffs. "There's barely enough for us."

His daughter has much to learn.

"It'll soon be full moon," the girl says.

"Don't worry," Father reassures, "it's only a problem if the moon turns red and that won't happen."

Maysu looks up at the gloomy sky.

It has been a century since the last red moon but many are still superstitious.

Father and daughter collect their bundles of coiled vegetation and set off walking towards the village. Maysu looks forward to seeing her mother's face. She will be pleased with their day's gatherings. They'll have Gringrow plaits for tea with salt granola. Her mouth waters at the thought.

As they walk she sees that the lake to the west is drained; nothing but fine soil, stripped clean of foliage.

Rain falls.

The lake behind them is bubbling as the Wingfish babble beneath the surface. They are agitated. Their gills click. The surface lathers as the mob gathers. They circle the largest Wingfish and 'he' sweeps his fins around him like a grand cape. His dorsal fin stands proud and erect. The others keep their distance. One blow of the tail and the sting would be fatal.

The females swim according to their instinct: drifting on their backs, stirring up the water with their floatier fins spread out around them. They nibble at each other with open lips and when the prima male shoots upwards out of the lake they are too busy to notice.

If the villagers were to stand on their roofs they would see the glitter of his scales flashing in the white of the moon. The village is built on stilts. Each dwelling has two rooms and in the gloom their tallow lights glint from deep within.

Mother recognises the footsteps of her daughter and husband on the ladder. They are echoed by a distant thump not unlike the rolling thunder that signals the beginning of a Soomoon.

In fact, the sound is made by the prima male as he lands hard on the shore.

Slap, slap, slap.

The vibrations ripple across the lake, girding the others into action. The evening is heavy. The clouds burst like ripe puffballs filled with watery spores. So much water fills the atmosphere that the fish can actually swim for short bursts of time in the air.

Mother calls out her daughter's name. They rub noses

150

for a moment.

"What would I do without my gatherers?" she says taking the burden of the sacks.

"So, how were the Wingfish today?" She casts a nervous look at her husband. "I've heard that the moon is on the red rise."

"Just gossip," he replies.

"I hope you left some Gringrow for the fish," she says, pulling at the stash of curly greens.

Meanwhile, the Wingfish are rising above the lake. The clicks are a drone increasing in volume. All the Gringrow that the girl and her father missed have now been eaten. The fish swirl hungrily around diving into the undergrowth but soon return, collapsing in the shallow waters. Even the prima male slumps back on the shore but underneath his glistening scales is a growing sense of fury.

Mother has the fryer ready for the spoils. Everything the Watterishi eat is cooked in fat or oil. It keeps their skins swollen with grease to keep out the constant damp.

Maysu looks at her Mother with her new coil. Her hair is interwoven with reed shafts and shaped like an upturned bowl. She will have no problem carrying the beans of the Ruba or their leaves that make waterproof tiles for each roof.

"Come on, drink up," Mother says, holding out a cup full of white liquid that has been drained from the bark. "It will make you grow big and strong."

Maysu pulls a face and holds her nose as it is poured into her mouth.

"Ruba is good for many things," Father advises. He has his teacher face.

"In the old days, the Wingfish were a real danger and the Ruba stalks were used to make catch baskets. Sticks of sharpened bark were tied to the open end; their arrowheads pointing inwards..." As if to demonstrate this he pushes one hand under the opposite arm.

"And if the Wingfish tried to escape..." now he clamps the arm to his side, trapping the hand.

Leaning towards Maysu he lowers his voice.

"The danger time has a name but you must never to speak of it."

He leans forward and whispers in the girl's ear.

"Soomoon."

Maysu's eyes widen. She is fearful but proud that her father has confided in her.

Mother puts an arm around her.

"We never have to make the basket traps now," she says.

From the horizon the approaching rain clouds sweep over the mountains. They linger at their apex before dropping their load in the far valley. The watercourses fill up to their brims until the mud banks begin to break up and slip away. The swirling waters form whirlpools that snap the delicate Gringrow from their roots. The fish are dragged along with the flow.

That night, all the Watterishi are laid on their Ruba mats; their bellies full. Dried Gringrow leaves rustle from the rafters lulling the dwellers to sleep. Silently, the waters rise up the stilts. Maysu leans out and watches the rippling reflection of the silvery moon.

"Soomoon, Soomoon," she whispers guiltily.

The girl's parents hear nothing. As the moonlight comes through the reedy walls it catches the oily glisten of the couple as they entwine and perform their mating ritual. By dawn their gleaming bodies are as slippery as the fish in the lake.

They awake to the lap of water slapping the underside of the dwelling.

"It'll soon abate," Father says, looking across the valley.

"Look how quickly it drains into the midden."

That day, the Watterishi glide on their reed boats, bartering and exchanging their goods.

Evening comes and the Wingfish have found their natural groupings. The clicking starts, louder now, as pectoral fins flap against hollow hungry bodies. Inside each of the females are eggs ready to be laid but the vital energies of the prima male are surging in fury at the Gringow stealers. The fish brush against each other and begin to glow. As the moon floods the land with an eerie pink, they rise in a towering cyclone, their scales reflecting a salmon tincture.

"The moon is turning. I know it," Mother says.

She is afraid. With the others she has begun to weave a catch basket but the stripped bark cuts into their unskilled hands.

High in the sky the orange clouds are torn by the oncoming winds.

It rains.

The men smoke their pipes and spit into the drains beneath them. The midden is choking with detritus. The men spit some more, the fish click and click and the women weave their traps.

The moon turns red.

The Watterishi hear the sound of snapping in the air. The women hunker behind their unfinished baskets as a blanket of darkness descends.

The moon disappears. Then the noise resumes, filling the air. The darkness has been a temporary shadow made by the swarming Wingfish. Ruby rays are filtering between their bodies. They rise up to the platforms, snatch at coils of hair, pulling threads of mats, flaying the Ruba roof tiles and stripping the dwellings clean.

Dawn arrives filling the land with a blood light.

The storm is finished leaving a hollow vacuum. The prima Wingfish is flapping on the ground; the blue light of his sting diminishing in the slip of the midden. The dwellings are stumps in the mud. Even the Ruba trees have lost their footholds and the lakes have melded one into another. Nothing is as it was.

And then.

"Kiri quar kiri," the call rings out through the raised land. A girl's voice.

Again.

"Kiri quar kiri."

From all around comes the sound of clicking. The girl points her finger and a loop of fish follows its course. Then, swooping simultaneously, they follow her command.

Indigo Dreams Publishing
132 Hinckley Road
Stoney Stanton
LE9 4LN
Leicestershire
UK

www.indigodreams.co.uk